THE BOOK OF THE SUMMER

SEASON ONE

EDGAR D JACKSON

First published in Great Britain in 2026 by IolandaPress
Paperback edition published in 2026
eBook edition published in 2026

A CIP catalogue record for this book is available from the British Library.

ISBN: 978-1-0683740-2-9

Typeset by IolandaPress

Printed and bound by Clays Ltd

THE MORNING, 18 JUNE 2073

When Daniel Ottoman woke up, he thought about his friends.

The sun was shining gently on the sweet pea beds, and the wind whistled past his window fleetingly, a hand reaching out of a carriage window to brush the hand of another. He lay in bed for several minutes and breathed. He watched a fly crawling on the ceiling above him and wiped his nose with the duvet. When he started sweating (which he tended to do at about eight-thirty, when the pills for his BPH needed topping up), he shuffled off the mattress and headed into the bathroom.

He turned the tap and washed his hands. Old hands. They were speckled with liver spots, calluses, and scars. Water trickled down the cracks and gathered in the nook of his thumb, and Daniel looked at it. A scar, sharp white, which hadn't aged a day. It was funny how they did that, he thought. Untarnished skin could wither and wrinkle, yet the remnants of pain stayed as fresh as the day they were inflicted. The memories were fresh too. For a second, and only for a second, Daniel allowed himself to be placed in one.

The memory itself was like dough. A tiny ball that could be rolled and stretched, until it covered an island. And so, while the remembrance was brief, what was being remembered was as long as the road to Castletown.

Chapter One

THE NOOK OF DANIEL OTTOMAN'S THUMB

The kids called it The Ogle House. It stood on Baltic Green, just up the way from Gorgon's Street, which Daniel often visited for sugar mice and gummy worms. He got them for a quid-fifty, a whole fifty pence less than any other kid, and for a long time, he didn't know why. But Mrs Margyle, the owner of Bennies, reminded him last summer.

Apparently, he'd got lost as a five-year-old during one of the church's nativity evenings. His mum had told him to sit at the front with all the other kids, but halfway through the performance, she had left to pick up her friend's son from the bus stop. Daniel, who had been looking back at his mother in two-minute intervals, panicked and went after her. But the sky had gone dark by that point. Although he knew the village, having lived there his entire life, he didn't know it would look so different when he wasn't holding his mother's hand. The houses were bigger, the roads twisted in different ways, and the moon — which Daniel had always thought he could poke — was a tiny, faraway dot that hardly provided any light at all. Being a smart kid, Daniel tried to get back into the church, but the doors were heavy. They could neither be pushed nor pulled, and so instead, he walked into the nearest shop with the lights still on. Mrs Margyle was washing the floors when he entered, and when he explained his situation, she sat him on the counter and phoned the police. While waiting, he was allowed to take anything from the shelves, and Daniel chose the sugar mice and gummy worms.

Mrs Margyle had remembered this. Daniel Ottoman had not. According to Mrs Margyle, this had also been the night Daniel had first heard about The Ogle. Perhaps to humour herself, she'd told him the whole story while waiting for the police. And maybe that went some way to explaining why the event had been scoured from his memory. Because any kid who had to learn about The Ogle at such a young age would be forgiven for trying to scrub the information out.

Not that information like that could be easily scrubbed, of course. Getting lost: evidently. The Ogle: evidently not. Daniel Ottoman wasn't sure when people started getting nightmares, but he knew for a fact, his started when he was five.

The Ogle was a creature that never slept. It stood seven feet tall (though a nerd in third-year insisted it was closer to seven-five) with a large hump and eyes that were twice the normal size. It had lived in the village of Deanshire for centuries. The first publicised incident took place in August 1869, when The Ogle was accused of killing a baby. A woman named Julia Hart had taken her two-year-old son to The Ogle House, back when The Ogle was a practicing physician. Rather than cure his smallpox, it had simply opened its jaw (again, twice the normal size) and stuffed him in its gob. Mrs Hart had said this in court, but because The Ogle's digestive system functioned at a normal human pace (which was probably the only human thing about it), there had been no evidence to bring to trial.

This story was hotly debated, however. Back in 1980, some fifth-years had been standing behind The Ogle while it was doing its grocery shopping, and they'd sworn they'd heard its hump whispering things. Their theory was that the baby was still alive and wrapped around The Ogle's neck, muttering instructions, which was why they saw him pick up a jar of sliced pineapples and buy seven cartons of milk.

One story took place on Christmas Day 1975. The Ogle had been visiting the local church, singing hymns and saying prayers like any normal Christian. Except the minister's dog, Arthur, saw through its act. While The Ogle was standing in line for a blessing, Arthur broke free of his leash and sank his teeth into the hem of its trousers. But The Ogle wasn't fazed. Rather than shrug off the dog, it picked him up, grabbed his ears, and pulled his head from his body. It then proceeded to drink Arthur's blood and proclaim to a shocked crowd,

'Not quite the blood of Christ, but it will do.'

As for how Daniel knew this was true, the current minster, who was around seven at the time, had told him so. He wasn't exactly the fanciful sort. No grown-ups were. And yet every resident in Deanshire had their own story to tell. Mrs Margyle included. On that fateful night seven years ago, she'd told him about the time The Ogle swept past her bedroom window. She lived on the floor above her shop, and when closing the curtains one night, she said she'd seen its figure, twice its usual size, crawling along the road and making for the hayfields. Frozen in shock, she'd then witnessed it crawling back five minutes later. Two badgers were in its mouth, and its eyes glowed red in the moonlight.

Baby-eater, dog-drinker, or badger-killer, everyone in Deanshire knew The Ogle was a nefarious, lingering entity that should be avoided at all costs, which was why Daniel Ottoman was so put out by the fact he was standing just five inches from its door, preparing to knock.

'Come on, Daniel. Give it what for.'

Daniel's three best friends were hiding behind him, peeking from either side of the garden gate. You could tell their personalities just by looking at them. Curtis Partridge-King, cool and collected; Manchester Harbury, maniacally cackling; and Jamie Watt, performing the Catholic cross. Daniel kept his eyes on them for several more seconds before turning back and clenching his fist.

The door was the thing. It was older than any door Daniel had seen, and so tattered that the paint was hanging off it like torn wallpaper. In the centre was a knocker, rusted brass, and at a certain angle, it looked like it had eyes. Two mouldy green spots that glared at him, daring him to use it. Daniel was still wavering on his first dare. He didn't know if he had the stomach for a second.

He twisted the cricket bat in his left hand and felt his fingers slip with sweat. Curtis had seeded this bat in the morning, in preparation for a game of cricket (of the French variety). Maybe The Ogle would see its reflection as the bat hurtled towards his head. Although if the stories were true, Daniel was pretty sure he wouldn't be able to reach that far, and he made a mental note, then, to aim for the balls, which were presumably at eye level.

'Come on, Daniel,' he heard Manchester hiss behind him. 'We haven't got all day.'

But Daniel knew that wasn't true. It was the tenth of July 2004, and school had just broken up for the holidays. Every kid knew how long that first day of summer could be. You could start with French cricket, end with an Ogle beating, and still be home in time for tea. And those were just the footnotes. No other holiday was the same. Christmas, Easter, the Autumn half-term. Those days started and ended just like normal. But all four of them knew that, as of yesterday, time had become a plaything made of putty. It bent to their will, to the point where, that night, the moon and stars would be blazing in a blue sky at ten p.m., and that would be perfectly usual. Because summer belonged to the kids. And kids wouldn't waste time thinking about it.

Daniel thought about The Ogle crouched in wait, its jaw touching the floorboards and its drool pooling in the cracks. Its eyes would be wide, watching the knocker, and its heart (if The Ogle even had a heart) would be beating in anticipation. Perhaps it knew Daniel was on the other side of it, his knobbly knees shaking like jelly. Perhaps the baby around its neck was whispering this information, staring at Daniel through the slits of the letterbox. Or perhaps none of that was true, and The Ogle was hanging upside down in the cellar, completely unaware of the lingering trespasser. That was a comforting thought.

'If you don't knock that knocker, Daniel, I'll dare everyone to bash your head into a tangerine.'

Manchester gripped his own cricket bat, which was now pointed at Daniel's face. In a split second of blind panic, Daniel finally relented. He leaned forwards onto his tippy-toes and gave the knocker a short, sharp swing. It landed with such a crash that the boys behind him gasped, and Daniel felt his breakfast regurgitate onto his tongue. He stood there dazedly and waited for his life to end.

Wednesday, July 11 2004

VILLAGE VANDALS STRIKE IN BALTIC GREEN

Two police officers were called to an address in Baltic Green yesterday to investigate a disturbance.

Upon arrival they found signs of forced entry at the property.

A local witness reported the damage was caused by four young males between the ages of eleven and fifteen, one of whom threatened him with a

CRICKET BAT. THE YOUTHS HAD FLED BY THE TIME THE POLICE ARRIVED.

RESIDENTS WITH ANY INFORMATION ARE URGED TO CONTACT LOCAL AUTHORITIES. IN THE MEANTIME, REMAIN VIGILANT AND ENSURE YOUR HOMES ARE SECURE.

'Can I frame it?' asked Manchester, holding the newspaper scrap delicately in his hands like it was a piece of ancient parchment.

The four youths in question were sitting in a treehouse, enjoying the shade on what felt like the hottest day of the year. All of their shirts were off, but even so, Daniel could feel sweat pouring down his back. He was a small boy with scruffy hair and twig-like arms, but it seemed he had enough water in him to fill an ocean.

'Why should you get to frame it?' said Curtis. 'I'm the one who cut it out.'

'Oh, well done. I'm sure it was really hard for you to use those scissors.'

'It was actually. Remember, I have special needs.'

'Very special needs.'

'Shut up.'

The treehouse was perched in the tallest oak of Curtis's back garden, just above the chicken coop, and they were lucky to have it. Two summers ago, Daniel and Curtis had thought it would be a neat experiment to kidnap one of the chickens and throw it out of the treehouse to see how far it could fly. It turned out a chicken with clipped wings couldn't fly far at all, though it could plummet to the ground, land in a water trough, and break its neck. Curtis's dad had threatened to pull the treehouse apart as punishment, but the chicken soup his mum made must have quelled his rage. Two years later and they were still thanking her cooking skills.

'I think I should get to frame it,' Manchester continued. 'I would've cut it out if my parents bought the *Deanshire Daily*.'

'What do they buy?' asked Curtis.

'Nothing because they're not squares.'

'His dad buys *Playboy*,' Jamie piped up. He was sitting in the corner with a *Sonic the Hedgehog* comic resting in his lap, though reading it seemed to be a chore, since his oversized glasses kept slipping down his nose. 'Do you remember? We found it underneath his bed.'

'Of course I remember,' said Manchester proudly. 'Where do you think we got Carol from?'

He pointed to a picture of a nude woman. Blonde hair, blue eyes, massive tits, nailed to the right of the entrance. All four of the boys had taken a long, hearty look at Carol over the years, so no one felt the need to follow his finger.

'If you want to frame it, you can go out and buy one yourself.' Curtis snatched the clipping back from Manchester. 'This one's mine.'

At that moment, Manchester and Curtis began their second wrestling match of the day (they tended to get about three in before sunset), and Daniel turned his attention to his thumb. The skin beneath the plaster was itching terribly, but he tried to ignore it. The bleeding hadn't stopped since the shard of glass pierced his knuckle, and he was pretty sure he was down to the last scraps of the first-aid pack. He could always ask for more, but Daniel was a lousy liar, and he had no idea how competent the police would be when looking for a suspect. Maybe they had seen the blood on the porch of The Ogle House, and maybe they would know it was the kind of blood that could only come from a thumb. If Daniel started shouting about needing more plasters, there was every chance it would be his name in the paper next time, and that would be a clipping worth framing.

'Okay, I call it quits!' shouted Curtis.

But the wrestling match had fizzled out already. Both he and Manchester could barely find a grip with all the sweat pouring off them. Recognising there wouldn't be a victor, they crawled back to their respective corners and tried to regain their breaths. Daniel pulled his attention off his itching thumb and repositioned himself on the ledge of the cut-out. He tilted his head and saw Buster, Manchester's dog, who was waiting for them at the bottom of the ladder. He was a brindle Boxer, a good mutt, and loyal. If he had arms, Daniel was sure he would've been up there with them, joining in with the banter or ogling Carol. He was one of the boys, alright — just with certain limitations.

Daniel gave him a wave, then looked out to the fields beyond, which were turning a little more yellow now the summer was in full swing. To the right was Curtis's house. A large Victorian property. Curtis's family was richer than the rest of the boys, but living in Deanshire, they were all supposed to be as rich as each other. Apparently.

'Do you think anyone would recognise us from the column?' asked Jamie. He'd given up on his comic book and was now sitting with his head in his hands, eyebrows creased, which he tended to do when he was worrying about something.

'Yes,' said Curtis sarcastically. 'Because we're the only four young males in Deanshire. Everyone else is a girl.'

'Man, that would be sweet,' said Manchester.

'I mean, do you think anyone else saw us? Someone we know?'

Curtis shrugged. 'Forget it. No one's gonna read this thing anyway. It's not like it's the front page. It's in the corner of page fifty. They barely squeezed us in.'

'Why *isn't* it on the front page?' Manchester queried. 'I bet nothing else happened yesterday.'

'There was something about the Deanshire cheese factory closing down. They're planning to build a supermarket there and people aren't happy about it.'

'I should have hit that bloke with my cricket bat. That would have bumped us up a bit.'

'I think you would've had to murder him to get on the front page.'

Manchester pursed his lips contemplatively. 'Maybe next time.'

'It's just,' Jamie continued timidly, 'I could really get into trouble if my parents found out.'

'They're not gonna find out,' said Curtis. 'And besides, even if they did, we had good reason for being there. The angle of this article is all wrong. They didn't even mention what house we damaged.'

'Are we sure we even got the right house?' asked Manchester.

'Maybe if you'd waited for the door to open before sending that cricket ball through the window.'

'I was trying to save Daniel!'

'From what? A draft? And you still haven't apologised for hurting his thumb.'

Manchester ran a hand through his long hair. 'If you were happy to stand there and watch your friend get eaten alive by The Ogle, that's on you. I myself had remorse.'

'You mean regret,' said Curtis. 'If you had remorse, he'd be dead.'

'And I didn't wanna let that happen.'

At that point, everyone in the treehouse turned towards Daniel, as if expecting him to interject. They usually did this when he'd been silent for an extended period of time. It was like they had a word limit set up between themselves. The moment they hit it, he had to slip a penny into the machine and then they'd all reset.

'Thanks, Manchester,' he said simply.

And then they started up again.

'So when are we going back there?' asked Curtis.

'You've got to be joking,' said Jamie.

'I reckon we let this blow over first,' Manchester said, like they'd just robbed a bank and were holed up in a safe house until their next score. 'See if the rozzers have any leads.'

'Tomorrow?' suggested Curtis.

'That should do it.'

'Why on earth would we go back?' Jamie gawped disbelievingly.

'Maybe we can send Jamie out there first,' said Manchester. 'Let him do some scouting.'

'Sod off.'

Curtis nodded. 'Or tie him up and use him as bait.'

'Yes!' Manchester agreed. 'We can send him as a peace offering. Say sorry for the broken window.'

Jamie jumped to his feet. 'Come near me with a rope and I'll punch your dicks off.'

Curtis laughed. 'Relax, Jamie, we're only messing with you.'

'I didn't know you could punch a dick off,' said Manchester.

Daniel huffed and gazed back towards the yellow fields. The sun was at its highest point now. Crevices and corners were filled with shadows. As the day went on, Daniel knew those shadows would grow — the ink of night spilling into the end of day. But for now, Daniel could feel the heat of that day burning his skin, racing his heart, until the hairs on the back of his neck began to bristle.

He turned back to his friends, slotting in another penny ahead of time.

'We're going back,' he said. And when they didn't say anything, he gave them a quid for good luck. 'I want to find out how the story ends.'

THE MORNING, 18 JUNE 2073

When Daniel was done with his morning shower, he dried himself off and slipped on a cotton shirt, pressed trousers, and loafers. Then he headed downstairs and filled Junebug's bowl with tinned sardines. It wouldn't be long before his cat returned from her nighttime hunting, but Daniel couldn't stand the smell of hot fish, so he made sure to leave it in the corner of the room, away from the sun. Walking to the kitchen, he made himself a bowl of porridge and took it out to the porch, placing it on the garden table before sitting down to listen to the birds.

There were three in full voice this morning. A pigeon, a blackbird, and a thrush. This was the way it normally was, but ever so occasionally, a soprano was added to the choir. A chiffchaff that perched on the nearest chestnut and sang until the clouds came in. It was a pretty bird, but a stupid one, and so Daniel made the mental note to check the garden for its carcass later — just in case Junebug's hunt had been more successful than usual. For now, though, he simply sat and enjoyed the bird song, being serenaded like he was the only person alive to hear it.

And perhaps he would have been, if a certain grey Honda didn't proceed to pull up in the driveway. It was strange, but Daniel had almost been expecting it. He knew there had been something different about this morning. The eighteenth of June 2073. The memories had been coming in and out in waves, circling around his head for no logical reason. Curtis, Manchester, Jamie. That summer at The Ogle House, where Daniel's story had begun. The whistle of the wind that had led him to this house, this chair, this bird song. He didn't normally allow himself to be sentimental. He didn't look back on the past, he lived it. Everyone did. Every day. In every detail. Except Daniel's past was different, he knew. Even now, sixty-nine years later, his story was something new. Something special.

When the car came to a halt and the door opened, Daniel stood up from his chair and waved. The stranger who exited waved back, then retreated a step and opened the passenger door. To Daniel's surprise, his cat, Junebug, leapt out. Her coat was laden with dust, and a collection of thimbles clung to the tip of her tail.

'Is she yours?' the stranger called over.

Daniel nodded.

'Silly bugger was giving me the royal escort. Every time I tried to move her, she just went straight back to the middle of the lane, so I thought I'd give her a lift instead. I hope you don't mind?'

The stranger shut the door and gave Junebug a stroke. It was funny looking at him. He wore nearly identical clothes to Daniel's father. A loose-fitting tweed jacket, a flat cap, a baggy T-shirt. But the rest of him couldn't be more different. The man was around six feet tall, young and clean-shaven. His eyes were small, his complexion tanned, and he walked with the kind of strut that his dad would have scorned at. He presented that strut now, walking towards Daniel confidently and pristinely before holding out his hand. Daniel didn't take it.

At the same moment, the calling of three birds became four, and Daniel glanced towards the chestnut, watching as the chiffchaff landed on a branch and nestled into a comfortable position. He retook his seat and listened, and the stranger followed suit.

After a few minutes, Daniel said, 'You remind me of my dad.'

And the stranger revealed a small, toothy smile. 'Well,' he replied, 'perhaps that's where you can begin.'

Chapter Two

FORKS AND SPOONS

The tearoom was dimly lit and smelled like gingerbread, coffee, and tobacco. It was located in the heart of Deanshire's high street, just five houses down from the town hall. Beside it was a deli, a bakery, and just opposite, a pub. Daniel remembered his dad describing this part of the village as a 'chasm between one world and another'. Every summer, the pavement outside the tearoom would be bustling with a handful of ladies in fancy garb, light blouses, pastel twinsets, and court shoes, while the other side of the road would be lively with forty-year-old farmers, grubby and covered with sweat. He said it was like the book *A Tale of Two Cities*, which was strange, because Daniel had never seen his dad reading before. The only time he'd seen his eyes linger on paper was when he was signing something his mum called 'freedom papers'. After that, Daniel hadn't seen him very often. Only every other Sunday, when he would arrive at their door in his BMW and take him and his sister out for lunch.

This was one of those Sundays, and it was a particularly strange one, because while their dad would often choose the pub for food (a sandwich and Coke for Daniel, a sandwich and lemonade for Daria, and just a beer for him) today he had crossed the chasm into the world of knitwear. Holding their hands, he marched them up the steps — making sure to avoid the slightly disgruntled looks from the women outside — and sat them down beside the window. He put on a fake smile when a young waitress came for their order. Without even glancing at the menu, he ordered two sandwiches and lemonade for Daniel and Daria (they didn't serve Coke) and an espresso for himself. When the waitress left, he scowled and grumbled,

'Bloody forks.'

'Forks' was the name he had given to the inhabitants of the tearoom, while the people across the road were known as 'spoons'. Daniel had never quite been sure why that was, but in a weird way, it kind of made sense. Why himself, his sister and his father had suddenly become forks for the afternoon was less obvious.

'Okay,' said Daniel's father. 'You're going to tell me how school's going, then you're going to eat your sandwiches, drink your drinks, and then we'll leave.'

He laid out the plan almost to himself, nodding along as he did so.

Daria huffed. 'Dad, why are we here? This place is *illustrioos*.'

Despite being six years old and speaking with a lisp, Daria had adorned a false poshness that made her seem older than she was. She also tried to use big words as often as possible, although most of the time they were either used in the wrong context, or just wrong altogether.

'I just thought it was time for a change of pace,' their dad replied.

'But you love The Black Fox,' said Daria. 'And I love the paintings in there.'

'I know I do, and I know you do. But sometimes, a pub isn't always the best option. Especially with children. It's not always appropriate.'

Daria latched onto this new word quickly. 'The paintings are very *appopiate*. They're the most *appopiate* paintings I've seen in a long time, and I like looking at them.'

'Well, why don't you look at the paintings in here?'

Daria spun in her chair. A single painting was hanging across the tearoom above a table full of old ladies. As if someone had simply snapped a photograph and slapped it on the wall, it depicted a table in a tearoom full of old ladies.

'Is that a painting or a photograph?' asked Daria.

'It's a painting, sweetheart.'

'Not a very *appopiate* one.'

Their dad chuckled. 'I beg to differ.'

At this point, the waitress returned with a couple of cucumber sandwiches and a jug of lemonade with ice and mint. Daniel was quick to remove the mint, and Daria was silently thankful. After a few more seconds, she returned with an espresso, and their dad drank it in one fell swoop.

'So, you guys were going to tell me about school. Daniel, I heard your grades slipped this year.'

The room around them quietened, as if everyone was suddenly interested in Daniel's academic performance. He slumped back in his seat.

'Not too badly.'

'They shouldn't be slipping at all. What's happening?'

'I don't know. Things are getting harder.'

'Harder how?'

Daniel shrugged. 'More science, I suppose. I've never got it.'

'What's to get? You boil water, it gets hot. The sun comes out, the trees wake up. Seems pretty simple to me.'

'It's a little more complicated than that.'

His dad laughed. 'Well, you can blame the Americans for that. Ever since they started talking about going to Mars, science has been the order of the day. Apparently, our government is worried we won't keep up.'

'So they're punishing us?' mumbled Daniel.

'Not punishing, no. Just making sure our kids are better than theirs. They build supercomputers; we build super-supercomputers. That sort of thing.'

'What kid is going to build a super-supercomputer?'

'Not a kid. But you never know what might happen when you're older. If you get the science in your head now, you might be on Mars by the time you're twenty.'

Daria slammed down her sandwich. 'He can't go to Mars. Mars is in space, and we can't breathe in space. It's *inpractical*.'

'All the same,' said their dad, rustling her hair. 'It's important to learn.'

'You said that school was stupid,' said Daniel quietly.

'I never said that.'

'Yes, you did.' Daria backed him up. 'In The Black Fox.'

'Well, that's another reason we didn't go there today. It makes your dad say crazy things.'

Daria tucked back into her sandwich. 'I thought it was quite agreeable actually.'

They sat in silence for a few seconds. Daniel now had the distinct feeling that the rest of the tearoom was watching them. That wasn't too much of a surprise. His father clearly wasn't of their ilk. His T-shirt was riddled with creases, his trousers too, and his tweed jacket hung loosely on either side of his chair, two inches too low. He was a working man. A floater. He dabbled from one job to the next, and at the moment, he was hot from the fields of Fair Willow Farm, where he spent several hours a day tending cattle and wrestling with tractors. They knew he wasn't one of them, and although Daniel and Daria scrubbed up better, they knew they weren't either. It felt like everyone in the room was waiting for them to leave. Anything to make the air smell that little bit sweeter. Finely balanced. With less tobacco and more gingerbread.

Daniel's father scratched the back of his neck. 'Come on, then. If science is no good, what are you good at?'

Daniel looked down at his sandwich and shrugged again. 'I like stories.'

'Stories. Okay, what kind of stories?'

'Interesting ones.'

'That narrows it down. Have you read *A Tale of Two Cities*?'

'Have you?'

Daria sat up in her chair, suddenly excited. 'Tell him the story you told me last night. The one about The Ogle House. You never finished it.'

Their father glanced between the pair of them. Despite the fact his skin still had a shine of dirt and dust, Daniel could see a glimmer of excitement on his face. It made him look younger, in a way. His dad was only thirty-six, but as far as Daniel was concerned, he seemed to age faster than most people. Perhaps that was because of who he was. A man running from one place to the next, never settling down, and never letting time settle down with him. He was in such a rush and yet didn't seem to be going anywhere.

'You came up with a story about The Ogle?' he asked eagerly.

'Uh-huh,' replied Daniel.

'Did you write it down?'

Daniel shook his head. He watched as the excitement drained from his father as quickly as the espresso from his cup. He was old again.

'Well,' he said softly, 'it won't amount to anything if you don't write it down. If stories are what you like, write them down and get them on paper.'

'Mum doesn't like it,' said Daniel, a little disheartened by his father's sudden switch.

'Why not?' he asked.

'She calls stories 'fairy dust'.'

'What does that mean?'

'It means they're *inpractical*,' said Daria helpfully.

Their dad scoffed, then leaned in towards the pair of them. 'Should I tell you a secret? The reason we're in here is because your mother doesn't want me taking you two to The Black Fox. This is where she wants you to be, and if she had her way, these are the people she'd want you to turn into. Snobby. Snotty. Boring.' He leant in closer to Daniel, whispering. 'I bet your Ogle story would scare the shit out of all of these prissy ladies who lunch, huh? And some of the blokes too.'

Daniel smiled and his father ruffled his hair, making it even more scruffy than usual.

'Write it down. I want to read it. And you...' He pointed at Daria, who was just starting the second slice of her sandwich. 'Don't fill up. We're just here to be seen. I'll get you a proper lunch at The Black Fox. We'll use the back entrance.'

They spent only another five minutes in the tearoom before crossing the chasm to the world of the spoons. Before they entered the pub, Daniel's father took him aside and told him not to tell any more Ogle stories to his sister. And Daniel agreed.

'Feeling my heart lurch into my throat, I leaned forward onto my tippy-toes and gave the knocker a short, sharp swing. It landed with such a crash that the boys behind me gasped, and I felt my breakfast regurgitate onto my tongue. I stood there dazedly and waited for my life to end...'

Six hours after their lunch at The Black Fox, Daniel was telling Daria her bedtime story. She was lying in bed, her hair still a little wet from bath time. In her hands was a teddy bear, and she was slowly but surely pulling the cotton from a tear in its groin. Daniel was sure it must have been a magic teddy bear with an infinite supply of cotton, because she'd had it since she was one, and she'd been pulling on that groin every night since. He'd been telling her stories for five years. Most of them were thought up on the spot, with no rhythm or purpose. Unlike real stories, there was no beginning, middle, or end, and no real plot or characters to speak of. He just plucked strands from his imagination, curled them into a ball, and gave them a quick lick of paint. Red paint, mostly, because he liked his stories to be scary. Daria didn't mind. She said she was far too *valyant* to be scared of mere words. But Daniel knew that was a lie. He could always tell how scared she got by the amount of cotton he found on her lap. He hoped one day he'd tell a story so good, her teddy bear would go totally flat.

'Two seconds passed. Three. Four. Then I heard footsteps coming from somewhere below my feet. They were muffled. Quiet. But definitely there, right below the porch, up some stairs, and phasing into my world. A door inside The Ogle House opened, and I listened as the footsteps approached me. They were loud and heavy. Not muffled anymore. I thought I could hear one of them dragging, like The Ogle had a limp. Each time it did, I felt the muscles cringe in my neck. My heart was beating fast. The footsteps stopped as they reached the front door, and I felt a million screams roaring inside my head. Not one of them was mine, though that was yet to come...'

At this point, Daria had pulled out a chunk of cotton the size of a golf ball, and Daniel couldn't help but smile.

'And then...' He stopped for dramatic tension. 'And then...'

'And then what?' Daria demanded.

'And then Daria Ottoman closed her eyes, squeezed her bear tight, and drifted into the sweetest of sleeps, full of dreams and nightmares.'

Daria shook her head. 'Only after the story is finished.'

'Nope,' said Daniel, closing an imaginary book.

'But you didn't tell me how it ends.'

'I'm sorry, you're just going to have to wait until next time. If there is a next time. Dad told me not to tell you Ogle stories anymore.'

'But you haven't told me any Ogle stories. This is the first one and he's not even appeared yet. It's just been you and your friends standing in front of a door. It's a bit boring, actually.'

'Tell your teddy bear that.'

Daniel picked the cotton from the sheets and squeezed it into his hands. *Must be around half a gram*, he thought. He always measured the success of his stories by the amount of cotton pulled from Daria's teddy bear. If it ever dropped below a quarter-gram, he would know he'd told a stinker.

Squeezing Daria back into the sheets, Daniel gave her a little flick on the nose (a manoeuvre he'd adopted to show his sister he loved her without having to resort to kissing) and turned the lamp out. The room was plunged into semi-darkness, broken only by the street-lamps outside, which would remain lit for at least another half hour.

'Daniel,' he heard his sister say.

'Yeah, Daria?'

'Did this story really happen? Or did you make it up?'

Daniel hesitated. His mind flittered back to the first day of the summer holidays, not two weeks ago. He remembered standing before The Ogle House, a cricket bat in hand and his friends hiding behind him. He remembered knocking on the door, and he remembered hearing the footsteps. It was a distinct memory. A solid truth. But not a truth that he wanted Daria to spread.

'Of course not,' he said.

Then he gave his sister another flick, turned on his heel, and headed for the door. It was strange, but for a split second, he could have sworn he saw a pair of feet moving in the gap between the threshold and the carpet. It was fast and silent, but real enough to make the hairs on the back of his neck stand on end. He kept walking either way, because he didn't want to alarm Daria, and when he opened the door and saw nothing on the other side, he passed it off as a trick of the light. He turned back to say one last goodnight, but even in the dark, he could see Daria's eyes were already closed. He made a mental note that the cotton must have been a quarter-gram, because clearly it had scared him more than it scared her. Then he headed downstairs.

One hour later, and Daniel's mother was racing around the lounge, turning over cushions and throwing pillows. She was wearing a fitted top and pencil skirt, cinched at the waist, and her hair was swept up into a vintage-style beehive. In the big light of the living room, Daniel could see she had lathered herself with makeup. Her wrinkles had all but disappeared, leaving a woman he would have struggled to recognise, if it weren't for the familiar chaos playing out in front of him.

'I swear every time I look for my keys, it's like I live in a mansion. Daniel, honey, can you take a look in the kitchen cupboards?'

'Why would your keys be in the kitchen cupboards?' asked Daniel boredly.

'I don't know, maybe they got hungry. Just look, please.'

Daniel's mother shooed him towards the kitchen, and Daniel did as he was told. He started at the far cabinet, half-heartedly scanning the innards. He found nothing but a collection of polished crockery adorned with flowers and hearts, with the big plates rimmed with gold leaf. That just about summed up his mum. To look in this cabinet was to fall into a portal, where Daniel and his family lived in the height of luxury. But to close it was to be placed back into a fifty-foot kitchen, beige and crumbling, with a pile of dishes left un-scrubbed in the sink. With a sigh, Daniel moved to the next cupboard, scanning inside for around two seconds before removing an opened packet of Ritz crackers. His mother raced into the room as he emptied them into his mouth.

'They're not going to be at the bottom of that box, Daniel.'

'You said they could be hungry,' Daniel retorted, spitting out a few crumbs.

'Don't be smart. I'm too late for you to be smart. God, this is just my luck. Why is it always the second date? First date, I can be late. Hell, it's fashionable to be late. Shows you're not too desperate. But the second date is all about promptness. Either you like the guy, or you don't. What's the time?'

Daniel checked the clock. 'Seven-thirty.'

'Jesus, I might as well hate him.'

'Were you late for Dad?'

'Thirteen years ago? I can't remember, sweetheart.'

'Were you ever late for Dad?'

'Daniel, please, I don't want to think about your father right now.' Daniel's mother picked up the bin and began rifling through its contents. 'How did your day go?'

'We went to the tearoom,' Daniel replied, moving his own hunt to the fridge.

'Oh good, I'm glad to hear he's branching out.'

'He said it was your idea.'

'Yes, well, turning his two children into drinking companions wasn't exactly what I had planned for his Sundays.'

Daniel's mum began picking up vases from the windowsill. She let out a high-pitched squeal when she lifted the centrepiece, and Daniel turned to find the keys to her Mini Cooper hanging from her little finger.

'Found them! Like I said, we're living in a mansion.'

Daniel closed the fridge. 'You wish.'

He didn't mean anything by it, but by the look of his mother's face, his words had struck a chord. It was like he'd poked something she'd been trying to keep hidden. Just for a brief moment, it was out in the open, investigating the disturbance. She didn't take time to dwell on it though. Shoving her feelings aside, she marched out of the kitchen and opened the door to the front porch.

'There's some leftover chicken in that fridge,' she said quickly. 'Peppers too. I won't be out long. I love you.'

Daniel leant against the banister of the stairs, giving his mum a similarly brief smile. 'I love you too.'

'Wash your hair. It's getting scruffy.'

And with that, she was gone, leaving Daniel and Daria alone for the night.

Daniel stayed motionless for a few minutes, listening as her car churned into life and drove away. It wasn't an unusual evening. His mother had been seeing new men for over three years now. But it left Daniel with an uneasy feeling in his gut because he'd never been introduced to any of them. None of them had stuck, so that didn't really matter, but Daniel couldn't help feeling like he was becoming a footnote in his mother's life. What if the next man she dated *did* stick? Would his mother stick to him too? Would she swing from one branch to the next and not look back?

Daniel wasn't sure, but he was afraid his mother wanted something more than what she had. Perhaps that was why she'd left his dad. He'd only been nine at the time, so Daniel couldn't remember if she'd given a reason. But there was every chance it had nothing to do with him, and everything to do with her. Maybe she wanted a better life. A cosier life. The kind of life Daniel's father couldn't provide. Daniel was only a kid, and kids weren't supposed to think about things like that. But he did get worried. Perhaps he and Daria were remnants of something that had passed and were on the road to being passed themselves. His mum didn't even read Daria bedtime stories. Though he supposed he should be grateful for that.

With a sigh, Daniel returned to the kitchen and removed the leftover chicken. He heated it in the microwave, making sure not to use the gold-rimmed plates, and then he ate it on his lap while watching television. After two hours, he could feel his eyes dropping, but he stayed on the sofa, adamant to watch as much TV as he could before his mother came home.

He only got another ten minutes before his eyes dropped all the way, and he fell into a dreamless sleep.

His mother was on the other end of that sleep. Daniel woke up to her stroking his forehead, her eyes glimmering.

'Hey Daniel,' she whispered happily.

Daniel blinked, bringing himself back into the room. He glanced at the clock on the wall. It was eleven-thirty. He'd been asleep for nearly two hours, which was strange, because he was normally scolded when he stayed up this late. But his mum was kneeling with a smile on her face, her skin sweaty and shining, and with a pair of red wine kisses on either side of her lips. She looked almost giddy.

'How did your date go?' Daniel asked unsurely.

'Pretty good.'

With a shaky breath, she lifted her hand and something white sparkled in the lamplight. It was a ring, large, with a golden band and a diamond in the centre. Daniel didn't tend to take much notice of his mum's jewellery, but he could see this one was new. He stared at it and frowned.

'What's that? Did he buy you a present?'

His mum nodded, and at the same moment, she broke into a strange laugh, choked with something wet. 'I'm engaged,' she said tearfully.

And then she pulled Daniel into a loving embrace, so tight he could smell the perfume in her hair.

THE MORNING, 18 JUNE 2073

A slight wind brushed the branches of the chestnut tree, and the chiffchaff tensed its wings. In the makeup of that wind, Daniel could smell blossom, grass, and a thread of salt, which came from the sea five miles east.

He hadn't grown up by the water, but Daniel swore he was made from it. Every time he saw the sun glistening off the ocean, or smelled the salt in the air, he felt a comfort in his heart that could never be matched. Even back home in Deanshire, he had never achieved such a feeling of belonging or serenity. It was like the waves of the sea echoed the waves of his soul. The same waves that had coursed through his veins for eighty years, moulding him into the person he was today.

'Tell me,' the stranger said. 'Why did you move to Cornwall?

'Cornwall's warm,' Daniel replied. 'It reminds me of summer.'

'Which summer?'

The breeze faded away. Daniel reclined in his chair.

'There were three...'

'Will you tell me about them?'

On the chestnut tree, the pigeon, thrush, and blackbird rearranged themselves, settling down on the same branch as the chiffchaff. The choir came together for the first time, and although they all looked different (grey feathers, black feathers, brown), their voices were perfectly entwined as one.

'I can tell you about the first,' Daniel said softly. 'But if it's all the same with you, I'll do it when the song is over.'

Chapter Three

THE MILKBOYS

The robin landed on the far-right tennis post and chirped for a while. Curtis eyed it up, one eye closed. He drew back his cricket bat, threw the ball into the air, and hit it with an almighty *whack*. The robin could never have seen it coming. Thankfully, it didn't need to, because the ball sailed about two metres to its right. All the same, it gave them one last chirp (perhaps bird-speak for, 'try again when you're in the big leagues, sonny') and then flew into the trees whence it came.

Curtis swore and grabbed another ball from his kit bag. It was approaching midday, and the boys had been hanging around the tennis courts for over two hours. Five years ago, that would have been impossible, especially on a day as nice as this one. But that was when the tennis club was in full swing. Every day, kids, teenagers, and adults would swarm the courts of Eastdow Meadows and play until dark, but when an overabundance of weeds began surfacing, the courts fell into disrepair.

There were some devotees who tried to summon them back to life. One summer, a poster went up in the town hall, calling on Deanshire residents to roll up their sleeves and become 'Weed Pickers'. They spent every Sunday on their hands and knees, pulling up weeds from the cracks in the tarmac. But the weeds grew back almost as soon as they were picked, and so Deanshire got more aggressive. The next summer, the poster changed to 'Weed Sprayers'; after that, 'Weed Killers'; then, finally, 'Dog Walkers'.

When the weeds won't budge, walk a dog.

Indeed, that was the poster that seemed to stick. It had been two years since anyone had tried to pull a weed, and while every dog in the village was healthier than ever, the courts had become completely infested.

Daniel lay in the midst of that infestation, propped up against the chain-link fence of Court Three. He watched as Curtis aimed his ball at some old silver tins. The tins in question were cans of Chappie dog food, fashioned into a pyramid. The dog that had consumed them (Manchester's brindle boxer, Buster) was nestled beside Jamie who was reading yet another *Sonic* comic. Wandering aimlessly around the court was Manchester, who had his hands in his pockets and was whistling the theme from *Ghostbusters*.

There was no question about it: the four of them were bored. Three weeks of summer had passed, and while the incident at The Ogle House had filled the first with excitement, the rest had been a dry slog where they'd done nothing but recount the tale. In many ways, it felt like their summer had peaked on the very first day. Now they were just hanging around, waiting for something to spark it back to life. All of them knew, though, that the flint wheel was back at that house. Behind the door they never got to open. Going back to it had been on the agenda, of course, but something was stopping them from making the leap. Perhaps it was because they were all too scared. Or perhaps — and Daniel believed this to be more likely — they had a suspicion they'd been lucky. Lucky that The Ogle's door had remained closed, and none of them had seen what was waiting for them on the other side.

And so they sat on Court Three, with nothing up their sleeves and nothing new to talk about, pondering what to do next. Even news of Daniel's mother, which he'd relayed in the treehouse the night before, had gone stale.

It was this news, however, that Curtis suddenly seemed desperate to cling onto.

'So can we go over this again, Daniel? How long has your mum been screwing about with guys?'

Daniel took a sip of his Coke. 'I think I was around nine when she went on her first date. So three years.'

'Damn,' said Curtis. 'She must have shagged all of Deanshire twice over by now.'

Manchester stopped whistling. 'Three times for me.'

'Sod off,' said Daniel.

Curtis struck his batting pose again, around ten paces away from the tins. 'And now she's engaged,' he said.

'That's what she told me.'

'Man, that's rotten luck.'

Curtis sent the ball flying high above the pyramid. He took a long, lengthy look at his bat, as if the problem lay in the woodwork.

'So what does that mean?' Manchester questioned. 'Are you and Daria gonna live home alone?'

Daniel frowned. 'Why would we do that?'

'Well, your mum has got engaged to this new bloke. Pretty soon she's gonna move out. I mean, I'm assuming the new bloke has a place. He's not some tramp she picked up on a street corner.'

Curtis retrieved his cricket ball and gave that a good inspection too. 'I dunno. Champ the Tramp looked pretty happy the last time I saw him.'

'She had a ring,' said Daniel.

'So?'

'So I don't think Champ the Tramp can afford a ring.'

'Well, that depends. Did it look like a ring you'd get at a jewellery shop, or one you'd pull off a pudding can?'

'It was a nice ring. It had a diamond in it.'

'That's what I mean,' Manchester continued. 'You can't expect her to stay in your sad old gaff. Not if this new bloke can afford a ring like that. She's gonna want to move out, and who's to say she'll want to take you with her?'

'Maybe because I'm her son?'

'Yeah, her son from a bloke she binned. Maybe she'll make it a habit.'

Curtis stood in position again. 'Leave off, Manchester. Daniel's life is miserable enough without you taunting him.'

Repeating his usual motion (ball ten inches above the head, quick two-handed grip, a mighty swing), Curtis hit the ball towards the cans, and this time it sounded good. The cans scattered into the weeds, causing Buster to jump and bark.

Curtis leapt into the air. 'BULLSEYE! ANDREW STRAUSS HITS IT FOR SIX!'

'Not bad.' Manchester walked up alongside him. 'Now let me have a go.'

'You think you can hit it for six?'

'I'll hit it so hard it'll turn into sixteen.'

'I assume you mean thirty-six.' Jamie emerged from his comic book. 'And that still doesn't make sense.'

'Just because you can't hit a ball to save your life.'

With a cocky grin, Manchester built the tins back into a pyramid, picked up the ball, and then proceeded to whip the bat into thin air. The ball plonked dismally at his feet.

'Hah!' Curtis laughed. 'All swing, no ding, I'm afraid.'

'I'll swing your ding in a minute.'

And then the first wrestling match of the day got underway. Daniel sighed and clicked his fingers at Buster. Obediently, Manchester's dog trotted up to his hand and guided Daniel to his favourite scratching spot, just behind his left ear.

Jamie returned to his comic and spoke without looking up. 'I wouldn't worry about it, Daniel. I've met your mum a few times and she's always seemed to me to be an affectionate person.'

'Is that a joke, or are you serious?'

'Do I make jokes like Manchester?'

Daniel watched the wrestling match go in Manchester's favour. He pushed Curtis down to the ground, kneeling on his back before pulling him into a headlock.

'I'm just saying,' Jamie continued. 'Mums don't leave their children. That's not something they do.'

'Yeah, well. Not every mum is the same.'

Daniel stopped scratching and rested his hand in his lap. This wasn't good enough for Buster, who proceeded to paw at his chest and eye Daniel expectantly. Knowing his tendency to bite when ignored, Daniel relented.

'You know,' said Jamie. 'My mum and dad fight all the time.'

'What's that got to do with anything?'

'Well, it's not very nice. It feels like every night there's something to argue about. The TV is too loud, the meal isn't cooked correctly, Dad's spent too much time at the pub. Have you ever tried to read while your parents are shouting to kingdom come? At least your mum had the good sense to put a stop to things before that happened.'

'Maybe,' said Daniel.

Jamie shrugged. 'I'm just saying, I don't think a broken family is measured in distance.'

Pondering this, Daniel turned and noticed the robin return to the post. It watched the wrestling match for a while, chirping gleefully as the boy who'd just tried to kill it received his karma. Jamie slapped his comic book shut.

'Hey, you wanna do something?' he asked, sidling towards Daniel.

'How d'you mean do something?'

'Get your mind off things. Bugger all to do here. Unless you fancy becoming a weed-picker.'

With his unoccupied hand, Daniel took one last sip of Coke, squeezed the empty can, and threw it at Curtis and Manchester. It rebounded off Curtis's shin, but he didn't seem to notice it. He was too busy trying to breathe.

'Look,' Jamie said, 'I don't know about you, but I don't want to spend my summer watching Curtis and Manchester throw handbags.'

'I thought you were reading comics,' said Daniel.

'It's the last issue. Next is out in August.'

Manchester yelped in pain as Curtis pinched him. Buster lifted his head to inspect. Sensing a window of opportunity, Daniel nudged him towards Jamie, who willingly took over the scratching job. Buster was none the wiser.

'How about going back to The Ogle House?'

If Daniel hadn't just finished his Coke, he was sure he would have spat it out. 'The Ogle House? I thought you hated that idea.'

'I did. Two weeks ago. But I saw something three days back that made me change my mind. You know I do a milk run on Sunday mornings? The route takes me through East Street, down Baker's Cross and then up past Baltic Green. Well, normally I take Tinkerberry Lane to avoid passing The Ogle House. But last Sunday, I changed my mind. I dunno, I guess I was curious. I took a quick glance while passing the gate.'

'And?'

'And the window Manchester smashed is still broken. Even the glass is still on the porch. Bet you anything your blood's there too.'

'So?'

'So it's been two weeks. You don't think The Ogle would've fixed it by now? You don't think he would've cleared the glass from his porch? I don't think there's anyone in that house. Not right now anyway. And I reckon I'd be far less scared meeting The Ogle if I didn't actually *have* to meet him.'

Catching the end of this conversation, Manchester twisted upright. Curtis escaped from the headlock, panting on all fours. Jamie smiled, evidently pleased to have captured their attention. He nudged Daniel on the shoulder.

'You said you wanted to know how the story ends...'

And then the robin disappeared from the post again.

The plan was simple. Daniel and Curtis would cycle to Jamie's house by eight in the morning, then follow him on his milk round to Baltic Green. Meanwhile, Manchester would be scouting The Ogle House, watching for any sign of movement. Upon arrival, the four of them would take it in turns to knock on the door, milk bottles in hand. If The Ogle answered (and gave them time to explain themselves) they'd claim to be new recruits who'd simply got the wrong house. If The Ogle didn't answer by the fourth knock, it meant the coast was clear for them to break in.

The plan for that was simple too. Manchester had already broken one pane of the front window. If they broke two more, that would make it wide enough to fit an obliging Buster through. Buster hated strangers, so the first thing he'd do upon spotting The Ogle (if it gave him time before it ripped his head off) would be to bark and notify them. If there was no barking within two minutes, five more panes would be broken and they'd all enter. That was at least £500 more in property damage, but what was a few more quid between friends? This was a once in a lifetime opportunity, and while it put all of their lives at risk, it would be a great story to return to school with.

As Daniel waited outside the Watt property, he wondered how he'd tell it. Jamie lived in the lower end of Hallow Down, which was the less glamorous part of the village. It was filled with small, crumbling buildings that looked like they hadn't received a spot of TLC since the early 1900s. His family didn't appear to be poor. Most of the time, Jamie was being dragged from one flashy social to the next, but Daniel knew they were the kind of family that were happy to be the guests and never the hosts. Like his own mother, a lot of effort was put into fitting in and becoming one with the village, but if anyone cared to look a little deeper, they'd realise it was all a facade. The hair gel was Brylcreem, the fancy shoes were from charity, and their expensive car, which could pass as a Porsche at a quick glance, was really just a Volkswagen Beetle with some nice paint on top.

Just as Daniel was thinking this, the door of that Beetle opened, and Jamie climbed out with a collection of empty bottles under his arm.

'Here we are,' he said happily, placing the bottles into the tray of his bike.

'Isn't there supposed to be milk in them?' asked Curtis.

'Yeah, that's where we're going.'

'The farm?'

'Yes. I know a cow there. She's very friendly and she makes tea.' Jamie pushed his bike onto the pavement and hopped on the seat. 'We're going to the grocer, you muppet.'

The grocer in question was on the high street, just five houses down from the tearoom. They'd been delivering milk since the early 1930s, and while it wasn't the most popular service in 2004, they still had a solid six customers to supply. It was run by Mr

Rosetta, his wife, and their eighteen-year-old son. It was the son who greeted the three of them at the door. After a brief query about why two other lads had joined the expedition, he filled the six bottles with the morning's milk, gave Jamie his fiver, which he would use to buy comics, and sent them on their way.

They didn't come across many village-folk on the trip. They glided through Deanshire quietly, just a few more summer leaves floating on the breeze, and it was only when they arrived at Baltic Green and the roads turned into rough country lanes that they dismounted their bikes and started talking.

'So, if The Ogle isn't there, how come Daniel heard footsteps?'

The question was asked by Curtis, who was already starting to sweat in the early morning sun. Curtis was a big lad, at least two inches taller than the rest of them, but his tall and broad exterior couldn't hide the trepidation in his voice.

'Daniel didn't hear footsteps,' Jamie replied confidently. 'It was a figment of his imagination.'

'Don't you think I get a say in that?' said Daniel defensively.

'No, because you'd probably say otherwise. When you're afraid, your brain tries to make sense of the fear by filling in the blanks. It creates patterns, explanations, to justify the feeling of danger. And when it doesn't have any real information, it just makes something up. Haven't you ever heard something go bump in the night?'

'Yeah,' replied Curtis. 'But most of the time it's my dad dropping his beer after falling asleep on the couch.'

'But your brain tells you otherwise, right? Sometimes it tells you that there's a monster under the bed, or some stranger hiding in the cupboard. That's because it's trying to keep you safe. It assumes the worst so you're ready for it.'

Curtis chuckled, lifting his bike as they traversed over a patch of rocks. 'Did you read this in one of your comics?'

'No. *The Perception of the Visual World* by James J. Gibson. I had a few weeks before the latest issue.'

Daniel kept his bike on the ground, noting the fact both his tyres were already halfway flat. 'I think I heard footsteps,' he mumbled under his breath.

'And what do you use to think? Your brain.'

'Maybe you do,' said Curtis. 'But most of us mere mortals think with our arses.'

'Give yourselves credit. Do you think I'd be friends with people of such low intelligence? I think all four of us are pretty smart —'

At that moment, Manchester jumped out of the bushes in front of them, cricket bat in hand. His face was covered in mud, and his clothes were soaking wet.

'HEY DICKHEADS!'

'Did I say four?' said Jamie, scratching his chin. 'Maybe maths isn't my strong suit.'

'What happened to you?' asked Curtis.

Buster followed after his owner, his coat wet and dirty, which he demonstrated by shaking himself down and giving them all a morning soak. Manchester removed a roll of fruit pastilles from his pocket.

'Had an Indiana Jones moment. Turns out Buster doesn't like The Ogle House any more than we do. Took one look at the place and scarpered.'

He stuffed three of the pastels in his mouth. Yellow, orange, red. Then he tossed another up in the air for Buster, who caught and swallowed it whole.

'Where did he bugger off too?' asked Jamie. 'The sea?'

'No, just the banks near Wealding Woods. There's a stream down there.'

'So you've not been watching The Ogle House?' asked Daniel.

'Oh, sure. I took one eye out and put it on the gate.' He pointed at his left eye. 'This one's my spare.'

'Very funny,' said Jamie. 'Look, let's get a move on. This milk's getting warm and if I want to earn my fiver, I do actually have to deliver it.'

He pushed his bike up the muddy path and the rest of them followed. First stop: The Ogle House. Then six more: Mrs Huckleberry, Mr Willis, Mrs Wilkes, Mr Johnson, Mr Slough, and Mrs Harper. All of whom had a cup of tea at stake.

It was a strange sort of morning.

The Ogle House was just as Daniel remembered it. A large oak tree cast it in shadow, but the darkness of the place felt unnatural, as though the house itself pulled the sunlight away. It was like one of those bruises you couldn't pinpoint. Some bruises appeared out of nowhere and for no real reason, and The Ogle House was one of those. A mark on Deanshire that no one could explain. Except this was a mark that lingered, that ate into the flesh of the village until it became part of its makeup. And like any other deep, aching bruise, it was better not to touch it.

Yet that was just what Daniel was about to do. The four boys walked cautiously towards the gate, and as they did so, Daniel noticed the glass on the porch. Some of the shards were still tinted with blood, sparkling in the light that squeezed through the gaps of the pergola.

'Come on, you stupid mutt.' Manchester heaved Buster forwards, his fingers wrapped underneath his collar.

'Maybe it's a sign,' mumbled Jamie, who had suddenly grown a little paler now The Ogle House was in sight. 'Do you think we should listen to him?'

Giving up on the tug of war, Manchester shoved his cricket bat under his armpit and grabbed Buster in both arms. 'Are you stupid? Buster eats shit, and I ain't gonna be doing that.'

'Really?' said Curtis. 'You spout enough of it.'

'Eat shit.'

Buster wriggled desperately, but when Manchester began tickling behind his ear (somewhat aggressively, it had to be said), he decided hanging around a little while longer wouldn't be the worst thing in the world.

'Okay,' said Manchester. 'I got him. Daniel, you go first.'

Daniel nodded hesitantly and took the milk bottles from Jamie. He waited for a whole minute after knocking the door, then he retreated and gave the bottles to Manchester. Like a relay team, this continued until they got to Jamie, who, although he had now gone about as pale as the milk he was holding, provided the final knock before beckoning them over.

When they got to the porch, Buster looked like he was going through an exorcism. He squirmed incessantly in Manchester's arms, and no matter how hard Manchester tickled, nothing seemed to do the trick.

'Jesus!' Manchester squeezed his dog as tight as he could. 'We're never gonna get him through the window like this.'

'Maybe give him some milk,' suggested Curtis.

'He's not a baby.'

'He's acting like a baby.'

'You're not giving him milk,' Jamie interjected. 'Like I told you before, I need to deliver it.'

Curtis shrugged. 'I'm sure no one will notice a few gulps missing.'

'The seal will be open, you prick. And then what will I say? Sorry Mrs Huckleberry, you're gonna have one less tea because I gave some of your milk to a demented dog.'

Having an argument on The Ogle's doorstep wasn't quite how Daniel had envisioned this plan working out. Even the door itself appeared to be mocking them, the tear in the paint stretching like a grin, and the eyes on the knocker seeming to say: *Really? You guys?*

'Look,' he said, wrapping an arm around Buster's hind legs. 'Let's just get him in there and do it now. He'll calm down once he's in.'

Aiding Manchester to the window, the pair of them lifted Buster towards the break and tried to squeeze him inside. After a few seconds of grappling, he fell butt-first through the gap, dislodging a few more chunks of glass as he did so.

Then there was silence. The four boys breathed lightly, their ears prickling. Even though it was broken, they couldn't see anything through the window. Only blackness. It was perfectly possible to bend over and take a closer look, but none of them wanted to do that. Knocking on an opaque door was one thing, but a broken window was like a tear in a shield. Possible to look into and out of. Now Buster was gone, none of them wanted to get close. And so they stood, and they listened, waiting for the faintest sign of a bark. Only none came. One minute passed. Two minutes. Three. They heard nothing but the sound of Buster sniffing around, with his small, leathery paws scuffling loudly across the floorboards. Eventually, it was Curtis who made the call.

'I reckon we should go in,' he whispered, though he didn't sound so sure.

'Perhaps we should wait a little longer,' said Jamie. His arms were still wrapped around the milk bottles, but he didn't seem so worried about them getting warm in the sun anymore.

Manchester removed the bat from beneath his armpit. 'If there was something there, he would have barked. You saw how he was. Dizzy as a Dodo. I've never seen him like that before.'

'Dodos weren't dizzy,' Jamie responded, as if that helped things. 'They were actually pretty well oriented.'

'Hold on.' Daniel glanced towards the door, slowly but surely coming to realise something. 'We've knocked this door at least twenty times. Once three weeks ago, and four times each today. But none of us have actually tried it yet...'

The four of them stared at the door for a few moments. None of them moved an inch, and so Daniel took it upon himself. He walked back onto the porch, the soles of his shoes crunching against the bloody shards of glass. He hesitated. Then, with a slight breath, he placed his hand on the knob, twisted, pushed, and felt the door move with him. A sheet of dust lifted into the warm, summer breeze. Like the gap in the window, darkness lay beyond. All Daniel could see were vague shapes, as if he was peering into the belly of a storm cloud. It seemed to take an age for the daylight to creep in, but when it did, and Daniel's eyes adjusted, he could at least make something out. At the end of the hallway, dead in the centre, Daniel could see the bright, shining eyes of Buster, who was sitting there waiting for them.

It was only when Daniel took a step inside that he started barking.

THE MORNING, 18 JUNE 2073

The birds had stopped singing now, but Daniel remained outside, his legs crossed and his arse beginning to go numb. He shifted in his chair and gave the stranger a slight smile. The stranger smiled back, shaking his head.

'You like leaving the audience wanting more, huh?'

Daniel shrugged. 'I suppose so.'

His hands fidgeted, missing the weight of a steaming cup of coffee between them. Daniel's usual morning cuppa was an hour overdue, and although he'd thought about halting the story several times to rectify this, he knew it would be an opportunity for the stranger to invite himself inside. If possible, he wanted to keep him out in the garden for as long as he could.

'Your friend Manchester.' The stranger straightened his jacket. 'He sounds like quite the character.'

'We all were,' Daniel agreed.

'How did you meet?'

'The same way every child meets their friends. The first day of school. Halfway between bored and terrified. You cling onto anything during those moments. A slight smile, a joke, a punch on the arm. Children don't survive on their own, they survive in packs. And we all knew it.'

The stranger nodded. 'So you found your pack?'

'Yes,' Daniel replied. 'Yes, I found my pack.'

At that moment, Junebug reappeared from behind the chestnut tree, a small, bloody vole hanging from her mouth. She placed it in the grass and sat beside it proudly, as if offering her guest a welcome present. The stranger didn't notice. His eyes were still glued to Daniel. Sensing he was waiting, Daniel sat up, trying to ignore the hollow feeling in his hands by placing them in his pockets. He cleared his throat, but before he could renew his story, the stranger lifted his finger.

'Can I ask you one more question?'

Daniel wavered. 'Go ahead.'

'Why go there? The Ogle House, I mean. If you knew what might be waiting for you, why go at all?'

'You're looking at it the wrong way. You have to remember; we were kids in the heart of the summer. When you're that age and the sun's shining, you don't bother with the *why*, you focus on the *why not*. Though we were terrified, not one of us could think of a good answer to that.'

The stranger's face creased in contemplation. Then, after a few seconds, he smiled like he understood and beckoned him to continue.

'So what happened next?' he asked.

And Daniel told him.

Chapter Four

THE OGLE HOUSE

When the dust settled on the porch and the light shone through, Daniel saw the blood. It streaked across the floorboards of The Ogle House, travelling in zigzags along the hallway and towards the foot of the stairs, where Buster was sitting. As Daniel squinted, he noticed one of his paws raised in the air, dangling a few inches below his chin, and dripping. He barked, then whined, placing his paw down gently before bringing it back up again.

'Is it The Ogle?'

Manchester was cowering beside the pergola, Jamie and Curtis behind him, crouched down in the long grass.

'No,' Daniel replied. 'He's hurt his paw, must have cut it on the glass.'

His friends rose slowly and approached, Manchester and Curtis with their bats raised, Jamie with the milk bottles still cradled in his arms.

'I can't believe it opened,' said Curtis, staring at the door as if this was some kind of magic trick.

'Doors tend to do that when they're unlocked,' said Daniel. 'Good to know you have my back, though.'

'Hey.' Manchester patted him on the shoulder. 'You can't have someone's back if you're not behind them.'

'Right, that's how it works is it?'

The four of them stood on the threshold of The Ogle House. It didn't look like much at first glance. The hallway was dark and decrepit, but not exactly what you'd expect from the entrance of a monster's lair. The floorboards were old, the wallpaper striped white and pink. On either side of the wall, there were three doors, one opened, the other two closed. On the ceiling there was a chandelier, three bulbs missing, and towards the end of the hallway, there was a thick, Egyptian-patterned rug that was frayed at the edges.

'Come on then,' said Manchester, giving Daniel a nudge. 'You go first.'

Daniel flinched as Buster barked again. 'Oh? You have my back, do you?'

Manchester nodded. 'We're behind you all the way.'

'Brilliant.'

Daniel stepped out of the light and into the darkness of The Ogle House. His friends followed in after him, keeping so close that Daniel could feel their breath on his neck. As they walked down the hallway, Buster put his paw down and stood, his tail starting to wag. He limped towards them and bit at his owner's shorts. Manchester leaned over and stroked his head.

'Oh, Buster. What did the nasty window do to you?'

'You should check if the glass is still in there,' whispered Jamie. 'It could get infected if we don't take it out.'

'Take it out?' Manchester replied, his voice a little too loud for Daniel's liking. 'I don't know about you, but I don't fancy losing my hand today.'

'So put a muzzle on him. You can't leave it in there.'

'Bollocks, it'll pass through his system in twenty-four hours.'

'He's not gonna shit out the glass, Manchester.'

'Guys,' hissed Daniel. 'Do you mind if you have this conversation outside?'

'Oh yes, sure,' said Jamie, all too happily. 'Let's go, Manchester.'

Daniel grabbed him. '*After* we've looked around.'

The relief on Jamie's face disappeared, the colour of his skin fading back to milk.

'Oh. Yes, of course.'

And then there was silence again. The four boys remained huddled in the middle of the hallway, facing out in all directions, as if The Ogle might spring from anywhere. For all Daniel knew, it could. Even the walls looked like they could be climbed into and out of, judging by the number of tears in the wallpaper.

Buster let out another moan and Manchester told him to 'sit'. Daniel turned back to the stairs, his nose wrinkling slightly.

'What's that smell?' he asked.

'Moth balls,' Curtis answered him. 'My mum uses a bunch of them in the bedroom.'

'Really?' said Manchester. 'Which bedroom? The master's or the servant's?'

'Sod off.'

'So The Ogle uses moth balls?' Jamie whispered. 'I didn't think it would care too much about the quality of its fabric.'

Daniel shook his head. 'We don't know anything about The Ogle. But we're about to.'

He moved towards the staircase, keeping his eyes fixed on the open doorway to his right. The room itself was empty. If it hadn't been for the paw prints in the dust and the blood that trailed them, Daniel would have guessed that no one had stepped inside it for years. Nothing living, anyhow.

'I say we go up first,' said Curtis uneasily. 'Work our way down.'

Not one of them could think of a reason to dispute that, so Daniel turned his gaze back to the staircase. Buster's blood formed a dark puddle at the base, and Daniel made sure to step over it as he walked up. The staircase twisted to the left, then to the right, past the old chandelier and onto a large, square landing. There were no trick stairs. No sudden morphing into a slide that swept them down to a pit of skulls. So far, so good.

On the landing, there were four doors: one to the left, one to the right, and two at the far end.

'Think we should split up...' said Daniel quietly.

'Don't be a tit, Daniel.'

Manchester pushed passed him and approached the door on the left. Giving the door a little push, Manchester flattened himself against the wall and waited for it to creak open. It was hard to tell what he was expecting. Perhaps The Ogle. Perhaps a giant pendulum blade swinging from the frame to slice his body in two. Whatever he expected, Daniel would have put money on a fine-smelling room filled with flowers being bottom of the list. But that's exactly what was on the other side. Squeezed into a small space were around two dozen pots, each of which housed flowers of all shapes and sizes, colours and scents, growth and rot. It seemed that, while one half of the room was thriving with life, the other was on the cusp of death. The four of them eased inside.

'Nice garden,' Curtis mumbled. 'Bit unusual. Been brushing up on botany between *Sonic* issues, Jamie?'

'Nope,' Jamie replied. 'Books about plants are boring.'

Curtis scoffed. 'But *The Perception of the Video World*, isn't?'

'*Visual* world. And no, it's not. It's fascinating.'

Daniel stopped at a green-orange plant and leant over to poke the soil. He then poked another one; then another; then another; and after the fifth poke, he turned back to his friends to report his findings.

'They're all dry. But dry plants can't be alive.'

'Alright, Monty Don,' replied Manchester.

'Who?'

'You know, the curly-haired guy. He does a gardening show my mum forces us to watch. Yammers on about orchids and daisies. It's a complete joke.'

'They could be fine depending on the plant,' said Jamie. 'But I wouldn't know.'

'Maybe you can add it to your reading list.'

Manchester patted him on the shoulder with his bat, then turned and left the room. The rest of them followed suit. It was Curtis who had the first crack at the next door. Holding his cricket bat tight, he turned the knob, kicked the door open, and did his best Andrew Strauss impression. Instead of flowers, the only feature in this room was a chair. Dark oak with velvet cushions, which was positioned towards a large, half-moon window. The window itself was covered in dust and grime, but even through the gunk, Daniel could make out a view of Deanshire. To the left, there were empty fields, and to the right, there was the high street. Beneath the window, there were a bunch of dying flies, spinning helplessly in circles. Manchester crept over and flicked a few off the sill.

'It looks out onto all of Deanshire,' said Curtis.

'What do you think he does?' asked Jamie. 'Paint us?'

'Or just watches,' said Daniel.

Kathump, kathump, kathump.

At that moment, the dying buzz of the flies was joined by something else. A dull thumping beneath their feet, which lasted for around four seconds before fading into silence. Daniel swallowed. He looked at his friends, wondering if this was just another thing he'd imagined. Judging by Jamie's face, however, he'd heard it too. And Curtis. Manchester, on the other hand, was still preoccupied with his fly-flicking. When he noticed their look, he shrugged and simply said, 'Buster'. Then he flicked the last fly off the sill and made for the next room.

This one had another chair, another window, square-shaped, and perhaps there was a draft, because all the flies seemed to be buzzing about the walls quite healthily. There was a clock on the wall, but that was about the only thing of note. Manchester made a joke about this being one of the worst museums he'd ever visited, and then they were off to the fourth room. The last on the landing. This one looked like the bedroom, with a railed bed in the centre and a dresser beside. Unlike any other room in the house, the walls here were hand-painted, with swirls of blue, red, and green climbing like vines up to the ceiling.

'What do you know,' said Manchester as they walked inside. 'Looks like The Ogle really is a painter.'

Although there was a window in this room too, it was a lot smaller than the others, and most of it was sealed off by a length of plasterboard.

'Hey, Manchester.' Curtis approached the bed. 'What does this remind you of?'

'Sleeping?'

'No, the actual bed.'

Manchester shrugged. 'I don't know.'

'You remember when we were playing cricket for the Under Elevens?'

'Oh yeah. You broke your arm.'

'Doesn't this remind you of the bed in the hospital? You know, the one you were messing around on?'

Although it was dark, Daniel could have sworn he saw Manchester's face stiffen a little, as if Curtis had touched a nerve.

'What happened?' he asked.

'Nothing much,' Manchester replied quickly. 'Built a fort in the bed next to Curtis. Only it smelled funny.'

Curtis laughed. 'Turned out the woman who'd been using it had died that same morning. You should have seen Manchester's face.'

'It didn't bother me,' said Manchester unconvincingly.

'I seem to remember you crying in the bathroom.'

'I have hay fever.'

'Oh, hay fever, is it? Those plants in the next room must be killing you.'

Manchester rubbed at his throat and feigned a cough. 'I am getting a little itchy, yes.'

'Bullshit. You were so upset you —'

KATHUMP! KATHUMP! KATHUMP!

The thumping downstairs returned, even louder than before. So loud, it felt like the house itself had a heart, with veins stretching behind the walls.

'I reckon we should leave,' Jamie whispered shakily.

Manchester smirked. 'Starting to regret suggesting this little adventure, are we?'

'No. We've seen all the rooms, haven't we?'

'On this floor, yeah. But there's bound to be more downstairs to investigate. Maybe even a cellar.'

'But didn't you hear that?'

'I told you, it's just Buster —'

KATHUMP!

Another bang. Jamie nearly dropped his milk bottles, and even Manchester grabbed his cricket bat in both hands. They stood in silence for a few moments, feeling like their senses had tripled.

'Okay,' said Daniel, giving Jamie a slight nod. 'I think we've seen enough.'

He crept out of the room and began walking down the staircase, and the others followed suit. As they descended, Manchester began talking about how to find the cellar in question. There was a movie he'd seen in the Urnfield Picture Hall, an old horror movie about a masked killer who had all sorts of secret rooms in his house, including one that could be opened by pulling a book from a bookshelf. He suggested they take another look in the first room, the one they had only glanced into. But when they got to the ground floor and saw what was waiting for them, they all went very quiet. Because sitting in the hallway, in the exact same position, with his paw still raised and his wound still dripping, was Buster.

The boys stared at him for a while. Then Jamie said something about delivering the milk, and the rest of them thought that was a grand idea.

Later that evening, Daniel stood in his mother's kitchen, scrubbing old sausage skins from an oven plate. It was seven o'clock, still bright outside, and he had the task of doing the pre-dinner washing up. He stood with his back to the door, the radio playing on the fridge, wondering where he and his friends went from here.

They'd left The Ogle House a few hours ago, their hearts pumping and their minds racing, but it hadn't taken long for the boredom to return. Rationality had been the killer. Something had gone bump, but things always went bump. And it didn't change the fact that The Ogle had been a no show. Daniel hadn't really wanted to meet it, but in a way, he'd wanted *something* to happen. Just to make things interesting. And now they'd visited The Ogle House (and likely wouldn't go again), the boredom was bound to get even worse. Like the weeds on the tennis courts, they could try to keep it at bay, but when the sun was hot and there was nothing to do, it would always return through the cracks. Daniel had been in a monster's lair this morning. But now here he was, scrubbing soggy meat into the kitchen sink.

He sighed and thought seriously, for the first time, about getting a summer job. That would certainly give him something to put his mind on. The only problem was that Daniel was eleven, and the job market wasn't open for kids who couldn't yet reach the top shelf. Maybe delivering milk. Though Jamie seemed to have Deanshire covered on that front. He could write a book, and that would make his dad happy. But Daniel had never put pen to paper before, and while his stories might have been good for Daria, they weren't likely to end up in the literary section of *The Observer*. Besides, there were plenty of stories about The Ogle out there, and all of them were far better than anything Daniel could imagine. He supposed the point of stories was that you made them up, but he'd wanted something real. Something that was true and exciting. Something of his *own*. But he had nothing. Just a house. Just some rooms. Just an ordinary summer day, where the boundaries were pushed, but not quite broken. Life wasn't a story. Not one that would sell, anyway.

'Have you been telling your sister stories about The Ogle?'

As if she'd been reading his mind, his mother raced into the kitchen and glared at Daniel with her hands on her hips. Daniel lifted his own hands out of the sink and scratched his forehead, which he tended to do whenever he was about to tell a lie.

'No,' he said incredulously. 'Why do you ask?'

'Because I just had a conversation with her in the bath, and she seemed to know a lot about that house. The front porch, the windows. And the last time you scratched your forehead was when you told me you did well in the science exam.'

Daniel shook his head slightly, dislodging a dollop of foam that had caught to his fringe. 'Fine. I might have told her one.

But there wasn't any blood in it. In fact, it was tamer than any of the other stories I've told her. Nothing happened.'

'You expect me to believe nothing happened in a story about The Ogle? That's like reading her *Little Red Riding Hood* and leaving out the part about the wolf.'

'It's true. Dad told me not to.'

His mother marched into the kitchen and picked up two plates of bangers and mash. 'That's probably the most sensible thing he's ever said, and I'll echo it.'

She dispensed a healthy dose of HP sauce on top of her sausages, then handed the other plate to Daniel.

'How do you mean, echo it?' he asked, following her into the lounge.

'Don't tell her any more Ogle stories. Not only are they inappropriate, they're complete rubbish. There is no Ogle in that house. It's owned by a Russian businessman.'

His mum put her plate down on the breakfast table, and Daniel did the same, flicking away some old baked beans that Daria had spilled this morning,

'Russian...'

'That's right. Russian. He works in tax. All that Ogle rubbish is just something the adults made up to keep children away from him.'

'Because he's Russian?'

'I don't know. The point is, it's stupid. And it'll give Daria nightmares if you carry on.'

'At least I tell her stories.'

'Yes,' his mother replied bluntly. 'Because you want to.'

Daniel slipped his fork into his sausage and began slicing it up. 'I know.'

They spent the next five minutes in silence, and when they were finished, Daniel took their plates into the kitchen and made tea while his mum did the post-dinner washing up. Afterwards, they returned to the living room to sit down. Upstairs, Daniel could hear Daria singing 'Ring-A-Ring-A-Roses'. He'd heard that nursery rhyme was actually about the Black Death, although he didn't know if that was true. He listened to her for a bit, then leant forward to grab the remote from the coffee table.

'No.' His mother took it from him. 'You're not watching TV tonight. That would be two nights in a row. You can do something else instead. Maybe go tell your sister a story. Something more appropriate for six-year-olds, with magic and fairies, and happy ever afters. You know, like the ones you used to tell her.'

Daniel huffed. 'I thought you didn't like stories.'

His mother shrugged. She was sitting in the armchair, her eyes latched onto her left index finger. Even in the low light of the early evening, her engagement ring was beaming, flickering each time she twiddled it under the lamp.

'I'm starting to,' she replied.

At the same moment, Daniel heard his sister finish the rhyme and fall down onto the bed, and so he climbed back to his feet and went to join her.

'Let me tell you a story. It's about a queen from a far-away land. A fair queen with dark hair, pale skin, and eyes the clearest blue.

She lived in a kingdom called Truth, a small but brilliant world which was held in the palm of an angel. When she was young, she was promised that she would inherit Truth. That she would live in the top floor of the highest tower and would be showered with jewels from the lost sea, diamonds from the glittering mines, and gold from the halo in the sky. She lived with this knowledge for centuries, because you see, a queen in this far-away land could live forever.

'When she was old enough, she married a handsome prince. A man with stark white hair and flowers on his crown. She gave him two kids, and both of them had white hair too. Just like his. They were happy. But on the seventh day of the summer moon, darkness came to call. A terrible storm, the likes of which they had never seen. A storm sparked by the devil himself. For the world of Truth was gripped in an arm wrestle. A wrestle between the angel, who kept this world safe, and the devil, who wanted it for his own selfish will...'

'Which was?' Daria pulled him out of the story. She was lying in bed, her wet, tangled hair making a damp puddle on her pillow.

'Uhh...' Daniel murmured, still in an overly dramatic, story-telling voice. 'Well, the devil was known as the One-Eyed Demon. A soldier of the underworld who had lost an eye in battle and had been looking for it ever since. For centuries, he'd been trawling through the darkness of the sky trying to find it, and when he saw this world nestled in the angel's palm, he thought he had. He grabbed the world of Truth and pulled, but the angel was strong. It pulled back and fought. It wrestled for seven days and seven nights, until eventually the One-Eyed Demon grew tired and fell back into the darkness. The angel had won. But this great arm wrestle in the sky had taken its toll. It had shaken the very foundations of Truth, creating fifty-foot waves that ripped the oceans, thunderstorms that tore the sky, and earthquakes that broke entire cities in two...'

'What happened to the queen?' Daria asked, her fingers twirling around the cotton of her teddy bear.

'She survived. And her kids too. But her beloved prince was not so lucky. There were many left dead and many never found, but the prince was the first. He was found washed atop a great mountain, sword in hand, as if he had joined the fight himself. And perhaps he had. Perhaps he had protected his queen and his children until his last breath. But the flowers in his crown had wilted. The Prince of Truth was dead, and the Queen of Truth was left alone in a world of ash and rubble.

'She mourned, of course. She cried. But over time, she grew resentful. Resentful at the lie that had been told to her so many centuries ago, that she would inherit this world and all the riches that came with it. Because what was Truth now? The jewels were drowned in the ocean, the diamonds were buried in the rubble, and the gold was hanging in a sky that had proven to be more dark than light.

'All that remained were her children. Her beloved children, yes. But children that reminded her of a time long past. A broken promise. So, one fateful night, she realised she had a choice. To stay in her broken tower and build a kingdom from the ashes or leave the world of Truth entirely. To set out into the sky alone and find a new Truth where she could start again. All she had to do was ask the angel to lower its other hand, lift her towards the stars, and blow her away like the seeds of a dandelion. She gave herself to the break of day to make that choice. And then...'

Daria sat up. 'And then?'

'And then Daria Ottoman closed her eyes, squeezed her bear tight, and drifted into the sweetest of sleeps, full of dreams and nightmares.'

'NO!' Daria fell back in exasperation, flinging her teddy bear across the room.

'You liked it, huh?' Daniel picked the bear up from the floor and shoved a clump of protruding cotton back into its groin.

'No, I hated it! I wanted The Ogle!'

'Once again, your teddy bear would beg to differ.'

He placed the bear back in her lap, and Daria pouted angrily.

'It's been over three weeks now, and I still don't know what happened.'

'I told you. I can't tell you any more of those.'

'But I want to know what happens next.'

'Nothing. I thought there was a story there, but there isn't. No fairy dust.'

Daria took this in, cradling her teddy bear against her chest. 'You shouldn't tell stories that you can't finish.'

Daniel flicked her nose. 'Note taken.'

Giving her a quick smile, he turned and went to leave the room. He glanced momentarily at the gap beneath the door, but there was no shadow this time. No anomaly. The light remained intact, and for the first time, quite assuredly, Daniel decided that it always had. He put his hand on the doorknob, but before turning, Daria called out to him.

'Daniel...'

'Yes, Daria?'

'What happened to the children? The queen's children, I mean. Not that I care. Like I said, I wanted a story about The Ogle. But since you told this one, I feel *obleeged* to ask. Were they okay?'

Daniel paused. He assumed 'obleeged' was meant to be either 'obliged' or 'obligated', but he didn't feel the need to correct her. She would learn soon enough.

'Don't worry,' he said instead, smiling as comfortingly as he could. 'You'll find out the end to this one.'

Then, with a goodnight wish, he left the room and closed the door behind him.

THE MORNING, 18 JUNE 2073

The breeze had picked up, so Daniel knew the question had been coming. The stranger was staring at him like he could tell he'd been dreading it. He was hugging his torso, as if to labour the point. Daniel nodded, standing up from his chair and stretching his back.

'Cold,' he muttered absently. 'Yes. Cold.'

'It's those sea winds,' said the stranger, standing up too. 'That's what I've found while being here. You can go from dying of thirst in the Sahara Desert to being halfway up Mount Everest.'

He laughed, but Daniel didn't join him.

'I wouldn't go that far,' he replied.

He turned to the house and noticed the watering can. He thought briefly about using it on the sweet peas, just to delay the stranger for a little while longer. But the idea fizzled out almost immediately. It could be now, or in three minutes, or five. It didn't really matter. The fact was, the stranger wanted to come inside. And sooner or later, Daniel would have to relent to his call.

He walked stiffly to the door and opened it halfway. The stranger slipped into the kitchen and patted himself down, and Junebug slipped in after him.

At least I'll get my coffee, Daniel thought.

And then he went to put the kettle on.

Chapter Five

THE MOLE

The goat shed smelled like suds and manure. There were around twenty goats inside, each cooped in small pens, glaring at Daniel with bulbous eyes that reminded him of oversized marbles. His father was sitting on a stool in his boiler suit, filling a large metal tub with hose water. Even in the shed, the sun was still bothering them, squeezing through the gaps in the roof to pierce any patch of unburned skin. Thankfully, Daniel had managed to find the perfect spot: in front of the third pen, which was covered in shadow, and just beside a crack in the wall, which was dispensing a sweet, easterly breeze.

'Pass me more of that shampoo, son.'

Daniel's dad pointed at a bottle of Hibiscrub by the tractor. Daniel sighed, stepping out of his shadowy cocoon and back into the light.

'Are you sure this is going to work?' he asked.

'It better work. I told my boss I'm a dab hand at washing goats. I even put it on my CV, since I knew he went in for these kinds of competitions.'

He was talking about George Carousel, the owner of Fair Willow Farm. He was the ten-time winner of the breed-judging show at the Summertime County Fair, which took place every August. Daniel unscrewed the lid of the shampoo and passed it over. His dad began pouring it in.

'I've lied on my CV plenty of times before, but I have to admit, 'Professional Goat Bather' was a rather unusual one.' He laughed and nodded to the first pen, where there were five goats still watching them. 'Okay, Daniel. Grab the halter and bring over our first client. The Fair Willow Spa is open.'

Daniel grabbed the halter from one of the hay rings and nervously approached the pen. He hated goats. As a six-year-old, his mum had taken him to Ringmere Farm to pet the animals, and while that was all well and good for sheep and pigs, it was rather hard to pet an animal when its head was digging into your ribs. The goat in question had head-butted Daniel so hard, he'd landed face-first into a pile of manure. He'd never quite forgiven it for that. Not just the goat, but goats in general. His mum had said it was stupid to hate an entire species because of one disobedient animal, but Daniel thought it was perfectly reasonable, especially since they all had the same eyes. Daniel had heard that eyes were the window to the soul, and if that was true, every goat was a head-butter in waiting.

Gripping the halter tightly, Daniel opened the gate and attempted to back the goats into a corner. This was unsuitable to them, however. They dragged him around the pen several times, from one corner to the next. His dad shouted over to him.

'Make yourself bigger!'

Daniel wiped the sweat off his forehead. 'What are you on about?'

'You've gotta make yourself bigger. Make them scared of you.'

'Oh, great. Do you have some growth tonic on you?'

'With your arms. Flap them a bit.'

Daniel lifted his arms and performed his best eagle imitation, but the goats were unfazed. One of them jumped into the water trough and sprayed him. The other goats began digging their hooves in the dirt. Fearing a head-butt was imminent, Daniel lunged for the one in the trough and just about managed to get the halter around its muzzle.

'That's it!' his dad cheered. 'Now bring her over.'

'I don't understand why I'm on goat-collecting duty. Couldn't you have done this while I filled the bath?'

'I could have done, but then you wouldn't be getting the full experience. Doing it yourself is the only way you'll learn.'

'Learn what?' asked Daniel, pulling the goat roughly through the open gate. 'I'm not planning to man-handle goats for a living.'

'You never know what the future holds, Daniel.'

Daniel passed his dad the halter. 'Okay, take her.'

His dad took it and wrapped his arms around the goat's belly, lifting it from the ground before placing it hoof-first in the tub. While this had been the goat that had jumped into the water trough, it didn't seem to like involuntary wetness. It began thrashing wildly, trying to get out.

'Come on, you bugger!'

Daniel's dad held on for dear life. He was being jerked around so violently that it looked like he was trying to quell a two-tonne bull, not a sixty-pound goat.

'I don't think she likes it,' said Daniel, trying not to laugh.

'I'm not exactly having a ball, either.'

The goat placed its front legs on the rim of the bath and pulled forwards, yanking Daniel's dad halfway over the edge.

'This damn goat!'

'Try making yourself bigger,' said Daniel helpfully.

'JESUS, IT'S GONNA —'

Giving one last mighty tug, the goat jumped from the tub and pulled Daniel's dad into the water. He yelled and spluttered, and Daniel keeled over laughing. His joy was short-lived, however, because it didn't take long for the goat to come back around and head-butt him right in the testicles.

They gave up on the bath after that. Once Daniel's dad had patted himself down and stood in the sun for ten minutes, he put the hose on full power and simply sprayed each pen in turn. Meanwhile, Daniel was in charge of shampoo control, which basically meant he had to stand on the gates and squirt in the goats' general direction. His balls ached for a good thirty minutes. At one point, he had to check whether one of them had been pushed up inside his body. He did so behind the baler, which was where he found the beers. Five Boddingtons, yellow, with barrels and bumblebees on them. Upon finishing the last pen, his dad told him to fetch them — 'which you may as well do, now that you know they're there' — but warned him not to tell his mother.

Resting against one of the hay bales, his dad opened a tin and then passed another to Daniel. At first, he thought it was something else meant for the goats, like the Fair Willow Spa offered complimentary booze after each wash-down. But he quickly realised otherwise when his dad raised his can in a cheers.

'Think you deserve that, buddy. Who knew that goats could be such hard work?'

Daniel hesitated. Then, quite slowly, he took a sip. He'd never tried beer before, but he'd always wanted to know what it was like. It turned out, beer was warm and frothy, and tasted a little like BO mixed with soda water.

'You, apparently,' he replied, trying not to grimace as he swallowed.

'How d'you mean?'

'Well, I doubt 'take your kid to work' days are normal here.'

His father shook his head. 'You know, if they did detective class at your school, I bet you'd get an A.'

Daniel smiled and waited for his dad to ask the question.

'I heard your mum got engaged.'

This wasn't really a question, so Daniel didn't answer it. Instead, he sat still and took another sip of froth. He held it in his mouth for a while, staring at the goats as they glared back at him, shampoo dripping ominously from their chins.

'Come on,' said his dad. 'Don't get quiet on me now. Who is he?'

'I don't know,' replied Daniel. 'I mean, I haven't met him yet.'

'You haven't met him? Typical. She gets engaged, and you've still not met the guy. Has she told you anything about him?'

'Only that his name's Rupert. And he might be rich, I don't know.'

'She told you that?'

'No, but he bought her a ring. A nice one. It had a diamond.'

'Well, he's one up on me. Best I could afford was a cheap piece of tin from a market stall. May as well have pulled one from a pudding can.'

'Is that why you broke up? Because of money?'

His dad blinked at him, then peered down at his mud-caked shoes. 'I don't know, Daniel. There were a lot of reasons. How long is the road to Castletown?'

That was something his dad said often, only Daniel wasn't quite sure what it meant. It was followed by another of his common catchphrases:

'You'll understand when you're older.'

Understand when you're older. Daniel hated that. He'd heard it plenty of times since his parents had divorced, and it was always a cop out. If he didn't understand now, that meant there was nothing to understand. The puzzle pieces didn't fit. Perhaps when he was older, he'd get a little smarter and stronger and might be able to force some of the pieces into place. But it wouldn't be a picture that made sense, and while he could make himself believe in it, doing so would only be for his benefit, not the truth's.

He sighed and took another sip of his Boddingtons. This sip was a little more absent-minded. He slurped it like a can of Coke, and the froth doubled in his mouth. It was the least he could do not to lean forward and spit it all out. Thankfully, his father didn't seem to notice.

'So, are you excited to have a new dad?' he asked, still staring at his feet.

Daniel turned away and squeezed his nose. 'Not really,' he said after getting it down. 'I just wish that things were normal. I wish we had a normal family, like my friends do.'

'Daniel, one thing you have to learn is that no family is normal. They might say they're normal, but they're not. Especially in this place, where there's so much on display. Pretty Range Rovers, fancy suits, tea sets and silver forks. Even in those big houses with all those rooms, there's always a key that doesn't quite fit in the lock.'

Daniel thought about that for a moment. 'Not all my friends have big houses,' he replied simply.

'Well, you know what I mean. People say that life isn't always perfect. The truth is, it's never perfect. And people who pretend it is are kidding themselves.' He gave him a pat on the back. 'It's okay that things aren't perfect. Just don't forget me, hey?'

Daniel looked into his dad's eyes. Maybe it was the sun, or maybe it was his dad's mild case of hay fever, but he could have sworn he saw something glistening in them. Surely not tears, because Daniel had never seen his father cry. But something. He knew because he'd seen it before, staring into the bathroom mirror and thinking about his mum. He could never quite hide the fact he was scared. Terrified, in fact, that she was going to set off on her new life and forget about her old one.

'I'm not going to forget you,' he assured him. 'Mum wouldn't want that, either.'

'I know,' his dad replied, his voice a little hoarse. 'And I'm glad she let you come out here today. It means a lot. Is Daria okay?'

'How d'you mean?'

'Has your mum told her about the engagement? Does she understand?'

'Oh, yeah. I mean, I think so.'

His dad finished his beer. 'It's her I'm more worried about. I know you'll always be my boy, but Daria's young and impressionable. Perhaps in a few years, she won't know that things were ever any different. What will that make me then, huh?'

Daniel remained silent. He twiddled his thumbs and rubbed over the cut, which had only grown redder since they'd visited The Ogle House.

'But hey.' His dad slapped his knees. 'That's a problem for the future. How're you liking your beer?'

Daniel nodded and took another sip. 'Nice. Frothy.'

'Don't tell your mother I let you have that, okay? In fact, I think I should take it from here.'

His dad took the Boddingtons from his hands, and Daniel let out a silent prayer of thanks. He watched mesmerised at how willingly he drank it. Perhaps beer was something that got nicer as you got older. Maybe that was something to understand.

'I'll finish this,' his dad said after wiping his mouth, 'and then we'll get back to work. We've got some cows to wash next.'

Across the shed, one of the goats yelled as if to say, 'good luck with that', and Daniel reclined on the hay bale, enjoying a few more moments of shade. His dad changed the subject and talked about cricket.

Later that night, Daniel was staring through the window of the lounge, waiting for his mother. It was approaching midnight, and the heat of the day hadn't dissipated. It lingered in the air like dust in sunbeams, hovering gently but never settling. Daniel was sitting on the armchair in a white vest and boxers, the television on, but muted. He'd been in the same position for around fifty minutes now, because his mother hadn't come home yet. She'd said she would be. In fact, she'd said she would never be home later than eleven, yet here Daniel was, his heart beating inside his throat, and the clock on the wall ticking closer to the dead hour.

As he waited, he thought of all the things that could be happening to her. Tied up in the boot of a truck, or crippled on the side of a road, her throat slashed. A dozen scenarios circled around his head, and while he knew none of them were true, that didn't stop them coming. Like this one: The Ogle. His mum had assured him it was just a Russian businessman, but how had she known that? If every adult in Deanshire had their stories to tell, how come his mother's story was so different? How was she right, and the rest of them wrong? Perhaps it was a shapeshifter. A supernatural being that could change its form to fit its needs, and perhaps it had changed its form to lure his mum. To make her feel safe, and protected, and loved, before its true shape was revealed. It wasn't entirely impossible. After all, what Russian would want to live in Deanshire?

Daniel shifted uncomfortably, wiping some sweat from his brow. Above him, he heard a door close, and his sister race to the bathroom. A few seconds passed, then the toilet flushed, the boiler rumbled, and Daria returned to her bedroom. The clock on the wall pinged. Daniel looked at it and saw that the mechanism was late. Two past midnight. They'd been alone for over six hours now, and the more Daniel thought about it, the less The Ogle seemed like the answer. All he had to do was look in the mirror, and he'd see it in his eyes. The same look his dad had given him. Except this time, the look would be justified and true, and that would make it sting all the harder.

He'd known this moment would come eventually. For the last year or so, his mother had been afloat in the ocean, connected to the shore by a rope. Her life as she had known it was there. Daniel and Daria too. All of them were waiting for her beneath the lighthouse, willing her to get closer. Only the current was strong, the rope was fraying, and all it would take was one big wave to do the job and cut her loose. Rupert was that wave. The ring was that wave. And while Daniel and Daria could shout and scream and wave their arms, with a current like that and a tired old rope, it was impossible to bring her back. Especially since she didn't want to be there in the first place.

Feeling his eyes glisten again (because sometimes he didn't need a mirror), Daniel reached over the arm of the chair and flicked the lamp on. At that precise moment, he heard an engine outside. A low growl, quite unlike his mum's Mini Cooper, coughing in the night and getting closer to the house. He twisted back to the window and watched a Jaguar pull into the driveway. His mum got out of it, and then a man, short and old-looking.

He was wearing a grey suit, shirt unbuttoned, and his shoes were so polished that they gleamed in the streetlight. They talked for a while. Then his mother gave him a kiss, a hug, and she headed inside.

The Jaguar reversed out of the driveway as his mother walked into the lounge, staring at Daniel nervously.

'Hey, honey,' she said.

Daniel didn't reply. He sat there with his arms folded, like she was an irresponsible teenager who'd stayed out too late after dark. She looked a little like one, he thought. Rather than the posh outfit she'd worn on the last date, she was wearing a loose-fitting top, ripped jeans, and her hair was pulled into two frizzy pigtails. She put her handbag down gently.

'I didn't think you'd stay up. Normally by this time, you're passed out on the sofa watching television.' She trailed off when she noticed the television was on, but no sound was coming out of it.

'I was listening for your car,' Daniel said simply.

'Oh,' she replied, nodding. 'I left my car at Rupert's tonight. Your mum's had a few champagnes.'

Daniel's mum stood in front of the armchair and gestured for him to move up. He did so reluctantly, allowing her to squeeze in beside him and wrap an arm around his shoulders.

'I'm sorry I'm late. I lost track of time. I promise I won't do it again.'

She held out her pinky finger, and once again, he took it reluctantly. After that, they sat in silence for a few moments. His mum was so close, Daniel could feel her heartbeat. It felt loud and laboured, and her breath smelled like alcohol. He pulled away and frowned at her.

'What's wrong?' she asked.

It was strange, but in that moment, she didn't look like his mother anymore. There were other scents noticeable on her face, in her eyes, even in the way she talked. She seemed happier than normal. Not in a drunk way, because Daniel had already experienced his mum drunk, but in a deeper way. A scarier way.

'Mum...' he said slowly.

She raised her eyebrows, mimicking him. 'Daniel...'

'Do you love us? Me and Daria?'

And just like that, the happiness wore off. His mum was his mum again. Even the smell of alcohol started to disappear.

'What sort of question is that for an eleven-year-old to ask? Kids your age shouldn't be thinking that.'

Daniel hesitated for a moment. 'But I do think it. It's your dates.'

'What about my dates?'

'You have a lot of them.'

'*Had*. I'm engaged to Rupert, remember?'

'My friends said it's not normal for someone like you to go on so many dates.'

His mum frowned. 'Someone like me...'

'You're not with dad. You chose not to be with dad.'

A few seconds passed. In the corner of his eye, Daniel saw a pop-up appear on the television screen, asking if anyone was there and whether it should go into standby mode.

'Is it your friends saying this?' his mum asked suspiciously. 'Or is it your father?'

'I didn't talk about you with dad.' Daniel scratched at his forehead, then shot his hand back to his lap.

'Liar. He always talks about me. What did he say?'

'Nothing. He just wanted to know about the engagement.'

'What are you now? His mole?'

Daniel didn't know what that meant. He wasn't blind, small, or furry. So he ignored it. 'I'm just saying, you chose to have our family like this.'

'Things like this aren't chosen, Daniel. Neither of us chose it. It happened, and we have to make the best of it.'

'Does that mean starting again?'

His mum's gaze flickered. 'Is that what you think is happening?'

'I don't know. My friends just say it's odd.'

'Maybe I think your friends are odd.'

'But they're right, in a way. Me and Daria. We're part of your old family. The one you didn't want.'

'Daniel, listen to me...' Taking his hand in hers, Daniel's mum pulled him towards her and stared him straight in the eyes. She was still and unwavering now, as if she hadn't taken so much as a sip of alcohol in ten years. 'A family doesn't mean a husband and a wife and their children. People think that's what it means, but it doesn't. A family is people. A dynamic. And maybe some people's families are different. Our family is different.'

'I wish it wasn't.'

'So do I. Sometimes. But that's okay. You don't have to be afraid. There won't be a new family and an old one. There'll just be us.'

Daniel took that in. Despite himself, he felt a sense of relief flooding through his chest. Because he believed her. She was his mum, and he believed her. But there was still one thing he wanted clarification on.

'So, if you didn't choose it,' he said quietly, 'and Dad didn't choose it. Why did it happen?'

His mother bit her lip, thinking carefully. 'You told me you've been struggling with science, right?'

'Yes. So?'

'Why are you struggling with science?'

'Because it's complicated. I don't get it.'

'And the harder you try to understand it, the harder it is to understand?'

Daniel nodded. In the corner of his eye, he noticed the television go black, and a red light appear beneath the frame. His mother leaned in and kissed him on the forehead.

'I understand you,' she whispered.

And in that moment, for what might have been the first time, it felt like they understood each other.

THE AFTERNOON, 18 JUNE 2073

'When did your mother die?'

The stranger was standing against the kitchen counter, a steaming cup of tea in his hands. Pomegranate-infused Cornish tea, with Cornish milk and cream. Daniel was sitting at the kitchen table, watching as Junebug rubbed herself against the stranger's legs. He wished she wouldn't do that, but the cotton of his trousers seemed to be particularly pleasing to her.

'A while ago now,' Daniel replied, taking a sip of his coffee. 'Twentieth of September 2055. Breast cancer.'

The stranger nodded, sipping his beverage and smiling down at the cat. 'She's an affectionate one,' he stated.

'She isn't usually,' said Daniel.

Growing a little fed up of her affection, Daniel *psst* her over to her food bowl. She looked at it and blinked. Then, with a pompous prance she must have picked up from her Egyptian ancestors, she trotted towards it and tucked in. The stranger made a funny clicking sound with his teeth.

'Funny puss...'

'Maybe we should stop,' said Daniel before he could help himself.

The stranger glared at him over his mug. His face looked dark, but it was hard to be intimidated when the mug he was peering over was decorated with flowers and kittens. Daniel had been given it as a gift around seven years ago, but of course, he'd never used it. This was its maiden voyage.

'What?' said Daniel. 'Am I satisfying you so far?'

'Yes,' said the stranger simply. 'But I know something else happened that summer. Something bad.'

'Ah. You want the good stuff.'

'I want your summer,' said the stranger. 'In all its forms.'

There was silence for a few seconds, but for the quiet munching of Junebug as she finished her bowl of sardines.

'Then I'll give it to you.' Daniel relented.

He took a deep breath and cast his mind back to the fishing hole, the eighth of August 2004, which was a Sunday with overcast skies.

Chapter Six

MANCHESTER HARBURY'S CATCH OF THE DAY

Manchester said he'd seen the trick in a *Simpsons* episode, where Bart Simpson tied a fishing line to his toe and lay in the sun, waiting for a fish to take a nibble. He may have missed the point, however. Never one to sit still for more than three seconds, he was currently in a sprinting competition with Curtis, the fishing line still attached to his big toe, cursing every five minutes that a fish had yet to take the bait.

The fishing hole was Deanshire's most frequented spot for anglers. It was positioned next to the old railway bridge, halfway along the River Rocker, which flowed from the springs in Rockerham all the way down to the English Channel. For as long as anyone could remember, all kinds of fish had been gathering in this spot, swirling round and round in circles like they were spiralling down a plug hole. Trout, chub, roach, perch, gudgeon, pike. All the English fish you could imagine were practically offering themselves on a spinning platter, giving even the most amateur of anglers a good chance to take one home. Sadly, while Manchester was a pretty good sprinter, his fishing skills were far below amateur.

'How long now?' asked Jamie. He was sitting next to the railway bridge, with Daniel and Buster alongside him.

'One hour,' said Daniel, checking his watch.

Jamie slapped his book shut and began drumming his fingers on the spine impatiently. 'One hour? Jesus. No fisherman must ever find out about this. We'll be the laughing stock of the town.'

'Do you know many fishermen?' asked Daniel.

'Not myself. But a group of them meet up in The Black Fox on a Tuesday. Carvery night. And they always seem to be laughing about something.'

'Heaven forbid.'

About twenty yards ahead of Daniel, a patch of reeds suddenly folded, and Manchester folded with them.

'Bloody bollocks!' he yelped, clutching his toe.

'Just give it to us,' Daniel called over.

'Like hell. If anyone's gonna catch a fish, it's gonna be me. I'm the one who had this idea, and I'm the one who's gonna be famous.'

'Famous for catching a fish.' Jamie shook his head. 'What are you aiming for, a Megalodon?'

'If it's in the fishing hole, you better believe I am.'

'Megalodons are extinct. What are you, a Megalomoron?' Jamie chuckled to himself, evidently pleased with his insult.

'Bite my dick.' Manchester came back with a rather plainer insult of his own.

'Listen...' Daniel stood up. 'If you want to catch something, you have to stay still. Let them investigate the bait before they take it.'

'Bollocks. I'm giving them a challenge.'

'You're challenged,' said Curtis, still panting from the last race.

'I'm just saying, there's very little chance you'll —'

Before he could finish, a murmur of voices arose from the woods to their right. Distant, incomprehensible, but slowly becoming voices they recognised.

'The Mumford Boys,' Jamie whispered.

Daniel felt his heart sink in his chest. The Mumford Boys were twins who'd been plaguing the village of Deanshire for over a decade now. Having arrived in the village as rowdy seven-year-olds, they'd evolved into seventeen-year-old vigilantes, known to everyone as the boys you had to avoid. They said they were from the north, but Daniel knew they had grown up in Grinstow, which was just a short train ride from London. Technically north, sure. But not enough to make their hard man accents any more convincing. Even so, they were a nasty pairing who'd made Daniel's life miserable at school, with never ending wedgies and beatings whenever they got him alone in a corner. Daniel had heard there was always a good twin and an evil twin, but Mrs Mumford must have been having a bad day when she'd gone into labour, because she'd popped out two of one, and none of the other.

He watched as the Mumford Boys climbed out of the undergrowth and came to a stop along the banks of the river. While Daniel and his friends had banked on a sunny day with T-shirts and shorts, the Mumford Boys were wearing black hoodies and trousers. They mirrored the dark skies perfectly, and Daniel rather thought that summed them up.

'Look who it is,' said Marcus, the slightly taller twin.

'If it isn't our favourite bum-boys.' His counterpart, Matt, grinned widely. 'Found a quiet spot for some fun, have we?'

Daniel heard a low, almost mechanical growl vibrate beside him. Buster had been spending most of the afternoon licking his bandaged paw, but his attention was now firmly on the Mumford Boys. He glared at them as if he'd received several wedgies of his own.

'Actually,' said Curtis, retreating slightly, 'we were just leaving.'

'Oh, don't go on our account,' said Marcus.

Manchester agreed. 'Yeah, don't go on their account. By the looks of it, they're the ones looking for a quiet spot. But it's okay, Curtis, we can turn our backs.'

Daniel swallowed nervously. Manchester must have received more beatings than all of them combined, yet he still talked to the Mumford Boys like they weren't a threat. The insults came like gushing water. It didn't matter that the room was flooding and the water was creeping past his chin, he could never quite bring himself to turn off the tap.

'What did you say?' asked Matt.

'Sorry,' Manchester replied. 'I forgot English wasn't your strong suit.'

'Just ignore him,' said Daniel. 'He's got problems.'

'No shit,' said Marcus. He marched down the bank towards Manchester, reaching inside his pocket. 'I think you forget, little prick, we don't go to school anymore. You know what that means?'

Manchester shrugged. 'You failed every subject they could throw at you?'

Marcus pulled a razor blade from his hoodie and grabbed Manchester by the collar. Buster started barking, but before Daniel, Jamie, or Curtis could do anything, the other twin was right there in front of them, his own knife raised and flashing under the sky.

'It means we have no one to answer to,' hissed Marcus. 'And no way to get into trouble.'

He placed his foot behind Manchester and pushed him down to the ground. He then climbed on top of him and began tracing the blade across Manchester's cheek. It wasn't deep enough to draw blood, but it was enough to leave a harsh red mark running from one side of his face to the other.

Daniel watched on in disgust. He remembered wishing once that he could assign the Mumford Boys a backstory. Like maybe they came from bad stock, or they were beaten as children. Anything to explain why they were the way they were. Only he couldn't. As far as Daniel was aware, they came from a perfectly respectable family. A kind Irish mother, and a little sister with baby teeth just starting to grow. The truth was, they were bad, and there was no reason for it. The Mumford Boys were bad, and they'd always been bad, and they would continue to be bad, perhaps for the rest of their lives, or until one of them was killed in a knife fight. And the other truth was, Daniel was glad. He realised one day, not so long ago, that he didn't want there to be a reason. He didn't want to look at them and think: if only this had happened, or that had happened. Because that would inspire sympathy, and that was something the Mumford Boys could never deserve. They deserved to be hated, because they were fixed points. A solid thing. And Daniel, indeed, hated them.

'Here's a little game.' Marcus looked up at the three of them. 'I'm gonna cut your friend here. If one of you takes a step forward, I'll cut him deeper. You move an inch; he gets an inch. You got it?'

He waved Matt aside, and his brother obeyed, lowering his knife and gesturing excitedly towards Manchester, daring them to intervene.

'Let's see which of you are cowards...'

Daniel remained dead still, watching as the tip of the knife breached the skin of Manchester's neck. His blood began to seep into the grass.

'I think I'll draw something,' said Marcus excitedly. 'You remember those old colouring kits you used to get as a kid? The ones shaped like a rainbow. I used to love those things, but the funny thing was, I never chose anything but red. I had a whole rainbow at my disposal, but red always seemed to do the trick.'

Manchester whimpered and struggled as another bead of blood slipped down his neck. Buster kept barking. The fact that none of them were reacting held him in check, but he was slowly getting the gist that everything wasn't okay. Daniel wished more than anything he could give him a kick up the backside and send him into battle, but the distance from his foot to Buster's butt was at least twenty inches, and that was twenty inches Manchester could ill afford to lose.

'Oh, and by the way...' Matt gestured towards Buster, clearly aware that the barks were growing more menacing. 'The dog counts too.'

'I got it!' Marcus cried. 'How about a name? Just a simple name written right into your skin. Because you've been a naughty little boy, haven't you, Manchester?'

'What the hell are you talking about?' Manchester winced.

'Oh, you think I don't know? You want this name to be a secret. But me and Matt, we hear things. See things too. Nothing gets passed us. Shame on you for trying to keep this name in the dirt.'

'I don't know what the hell you're talking about!'

'Try telling that to poor Cal...'

'Hey! Hey! Don't —'

Laughing away his victim's cries, Marcus began carving a *C* into Manchester's skin. The joints of his fingers bent and flattened as he turned the blade, almost graceful in his method. Daniel averted his gaze, starting to go a little light-headed. Just as he did so, something else caught his attention. At first, he thought it was a snake, parting the grass in the bank and gliding towards the pair of them. But then he saw Manchester's hand moving subtly from side to side, his thumb and forefinger touching, then parting, then touching, then parting. And he realised what was happening immediately. Slowly but surely, Manchester was pulling the line in.

'You guys aren't going to help, huh?' Marcus finished carving the *C* and looked up, his eyes flashing. 'Seriously, an extra few inches, and this will come out way better.'

The boys remained still. Daniel didn't know if Curtis or Jamie had noticed the line, but he prayed that they hadn't. They weren't good at hiding things, and given Buster was still by their side — albeit, bouncing up and down anxiously now — the fishing line was likely to be their only way out. He just hoped there wasn't a trout at the end of it.

Marcus turned back to Manchester. 'Some friends you have.'

He started work on the *A*, leaning in close and squinting a little, as if he was an artist working on a particularly delicate canvas. But before he could really get going, Manchester's hand shot upwards, and the painting came to a halt.

The next few seconds seemed to happen in one. Marcus screamed, clutching his eye as the knife fell to the ground. At the same moment, Buster rushed forwards, charging towards his owner before sinking his teeth into Marcus's arm. He screamed again and tumbled backwards, his hands peeling away to reveal his injury. The fishing hook was embedded inside his right eyelid, causing a stream of blood to fall down his cheek and curl into his mouth. As if aware this was already a man down, Buster rushed at Matt, grabbing him by the calf and yanking him violently towards the river.

'SHIT!'

Matt slashed with his knife, but he only managed to clip a few tufts of fur above Buster's collar. In retaliation, Buster let go and bit again, around the ankle this time. Daniel could have sworn he heard a crunch, although that might have been the sound of Manchester's foot slamming into Marcus's ribcage.

'YOU STUPID NORTHERN PRICK! YOU THINK YOU CAN SCARE ME?!'

He went to stamp again, but Curtis's arms were wrapped around his torso now, pulling him away from his victim.

'GET OFF ME!' Manchester yelled.

'DON'T BE AN IDIOT, MANCHESTER! WE'VE GOTTA GET OUT OF HERE!'

And then the four of them were running, sprinting as fast as they could into the undergrowth. Behind him, Daniel heard Marcus let out another yelp as the fishing hook was plucked clean from his face. He turned to see it snaking through the grass, still attached to Manchester's toe.

'BUSTER!' Manchester yelled. 'BUSTER, HEEL!'

Buster was still mauling Matt's ankle, twisting around in the reeds like a crocodile in a death roll. Matt slashed as wildly as he could, but the dog was out of reach, and after a few more seconds, he was gone completely, sprinting back up the bank to run alongside his owner.

The blood of the Mumford Boys was dripping from his chin, and it followed the boys all the way back to Deanshire's high street.

They sought refuge in The Black Fox. It was three o'clock in the afternoon, so the pub was busy, but most of the drinkers were out in the garden, taking advantage of the natural shade the clouds had given them. Daniel, Curtis, Jamie, and Manchester sat in the corner, just beneath one of Daria's latest favourite paintings — a blue spiral with a black spot in the middle. Daniel couldn't understand why she liked it so much (perhaps it was because all modern art looked like it could have been drawn by a six-year-old), but he didn't take time to dissect it now. The four of them kept their heads down, breathing heavily and staring out of the window onto the road.

They hadn't been followed. For all they knew, the Mumford Boys were still writhing in pain by the River Rocker. Or perhaps they *had* followed them, but since one of them couldn't walk and the other was half blind, Matt had given up, and Marcus had fallen down a badger hole. That was the least likely scenario, but either way, Daniel hoped they wouldn't come looking for them here. The plan was to stay in The Black Fox for at least an hour, nursing the drinks Jamie would buy with his fiver. Then they'd split up and make their way home. It was important they stayed together right now, around people and most importantly, around Buster, who was currently curled up under the table, calmly and contentedly licking the blood off his fur.

Daniel peered across the room and caught the gaze of the bartender, a twenty-year-old called Sam, who was distinctive for his long ponytail and thick Kiwi accent. He smiled at him and walked over.

'Okay,' Daniel whispered to his friends. 'He's coming. Everyone just stay calm and let me do the talking.'

Jamie shifted in his chair, repeating 'oh shit, oh shit, oh shit' constantly under his breath.

Daniel kicked him. 'Stop doing that. Saying *oh shit* isn't calm. Saying *oh shit* tells people there's something to say *oh shit* about. And we're just four kids visiting the pub on a Sunday afternoon. Completely normal.'

Jamie stopped just as Sam arrived at their table. He turned to give him the most false, painful smile imaginable. Sam frowned back.

'Everything alright, lads?'

'Oh, we're fine thanks.' Daniel tried to make his own smile a little more convincing.

'You waiting for your dad, little Ottoman?' Sam checked his watch. 'He's usually in by this point.'

'No, we're just thirsty. Can we have four Cokes, please?'

'You know, we're not supposed to serve kids if you're not accompanied by an adult.' Sam glanced at Manchester and his eyes widened. 'Oh, damn. Are you alright, buddy?'

He was looking at his neck, where the *C* and the half-finished *A* were still bleeding onto his T-shirt.

'Oh, yeah,' replied Manchester. 'Just a tattoo gone wrong.'

Sam wavered for a moment, and Daniel held his breath. He was almost certain that excuse wouldn't land, but to his surprise, Sam let out a great big laugh.

'I've been there, my friend. Got this one a few years back...' He pulled his shirt to reveal a tattoo of some coordinates on his collarbone. 'They're supposed to be the coordinates for my hometown in Auckland, but I guess I looked at the map wrong. Takes you to a fish restaurant in Sri Lanka. The reviews are good though. I looked it up.'

Daniel nodded sympathetically. He knew that Sam wasn't the brightest tool in the toolbox. Perhaps that was why he came all the way from New Zealand to serve beer in The Black Fox. But that was no matter, as it gave them a significant advantage.

'Actually, Sam,' he said pointedly, 'I *am* waiting for my dad. We all are. We're going bowling together, you see. He's going to be a little late though, so he told me to get some drinks while we waited. He said Sam would be happy to do it.'

Daniel stared at him earnestly, trying as hard as he could not to scratch at his forehead. A few seconds passed, then, evidently pleased that Daniel's dad had singled him out by name, Sam puffed out his chest and nodded.

'Sure thing, little Ottoman. Do you want ice too?'

'No, just Coke please.'

He pointed at Manchester. 'I meant for this guy.'

'Oh. Sure. Thanks.'

With a courteous nod, Sam turned and walked back behind the bar, leaving the four of them alone. They sat in silence for a while, trying to process everything that had just happened. The Mumford Boys wouldn't forgive them for this, Daniel was sure of that. If Marcus had pulled a knife on Manchester just for being a smart arse, God only knew what he would do after being stabbed in the face with a fishing hook. Daniel hadn't seen exactly how bad the damage was, but there was every chance Marcus would be waking up tomorrow one eye short, and if that was the case, this might just be the last Coke any of them would ever drink. He didn't like the thought of that, so he tried to place his attention elsewhere.

The Black Fox. A place where Daniel and Daria had spent many happy afternoons with their father. The pub looked darker now. Without his father in the room, Daniel could see the cobwebs in the corners, he could smell the dampness in the wood. Even the paintings looked different. Granted, two of them were on constant rotation — the one above them, and the one behind the bar, which was currently a portrait of a white-eyed man that had been staring at Daniel ever since he'd walked in — but the rest had always been the same. They were done by local artists, so they weren't exactly gallery-worthy, but even so, they looked rougher around the edges. Like this one, just next to the window. The canvas depicted a large, green field, with blue skies to the left and black skies to the right. Daniel had always thought it looked quite pretty, but right now, he just found it depressing. It told him that summer wasn't always treehouses and fishing holes. The remnants of winter remained, and if you taunted and prodded them, they would happily sprinkle some snow onto your luscious green fields. That had been Manchester's mistake. But they were all paying for it. The four of them were a pack. A line of dominoes. If one of them went down, the rest would soon follow.

Daniel turned as their drinks arrived — tall glasses of bubbling Coke and a pack of ice for Manchester, which he put on his neck for around three seconds before deciding it was too cold.

'The last thing I need is sugar,' said Jamie quietly. 'My heart's pounding faster than Sonic on steroids.'

'And me,' said Curtis.

He looked uncharacteristically shaken, which was strange, because Curtis had always felt like the leader of the group — mainly because he was the eldest, the tallest, and he had the treehouse. Right now, it didn't look like he'd lead them anywhere but the space under his bed.

'My heart's fine,' said Manchester.

Curtis looked at him indignantly. 'Maybe it's run out of blood to pump.'

'This?' Manchester flicked at his neck. 'Tis merely a scratch.'

He was trying to inject some humour into the situation, but that didn't hide the trepidation in his eyes. It was clear he was waiting for something. And even without speaking, Daniel, Curtis, and Jamie knew exactly what that was. It was Curtis who eventually asked the question.

'So who's Cal?'

Manchester's smile disappeared. 'Who?'

'Come on, don't be funny. The name on your neck.'

'Didn't you hear me? I have no idea what Marcus was talking about.'

'But he must have had some reason to —'

'I told you, I don't know what he was on about.'

Manchester's voice grew louder, and some of the heads in the bar turned. For a moment, it looked like the white-eyed man in the painting turned too, but Daniel quickly realised it was just his imagination. Those eyes were still on him.

'Anyway,' Manchester continued, 'why does it matter? Is that what you were thinking about while you were standing there *not* helping me?'

'Hey, what else were we supposed to do? Marcus told us what would happen if we moved. He would've slit your throat, Manchester. And if anyone's gonna do that, it's gonna be me. God knows, you've asked for it enough.'

'Yeah right,' Manchester scoffed. 'You can't even beat me in a wrestling match.'

'If I had a knife I might.'

'Seriously though,' Jamie cut in, 'what are we gonna do now?'

'How d'you mean?' asked Manchester.

'You think the Mumford Boys are just gonna forgive and forget? You shoved a fishing hook into Marcus's eye.'

'I told you I'd catch something big.'

'And Buster nearly tore Matt's leg off.'

Under the table, Buster lifted his head and gave a little whine of acknowledgement. Then he went back to licking the blood off his fur.

'So let them cry.' Manchester shrugged. 'It's not like they're gonna tell anyone. We all know what happened, it's on my neck to prove it. And besides, they're not gonna be around for much longer. They've got an apprenticeship up near London. I heard they're leaving at the end of the summer.'

'How do you know that?' asked Curtis.

'My mum knows their mum. Think she must have told me.'

Daniel felt his stomach drop. 'Then we're in serious trouble,' he said quietly. 'If they're leaving soon, then they've got a way out. No strings attached.'

His friends looked at him, then went quiet for a moment. Jamie's face became even more pale. Curtis's too. Manchester, on the other hand, gave a little chuckle and began fidgeting with his feet. They were still bare and caked with mud, and the fishing line was still attached to his big toe. He undid the knot and dangled it in front of his face.

'Certainly didn't leave this string attached.'

Curtis snorted, a little colour returning to his complexion. 'That was great. How'd you come up with that?'

'Well, Curtis. When you have a Mumford Boy sticking a knife in your throat, it does tend to focus the mind somewhat.'

He laughed and then, just like that, the pair of them fell into a deep, animated retelling of what had just happened. Already, it was like the last hour had fallen into myth and folklore, where it was just another story to add to the pile along with the falling chicken and The Ogle House. Only Daniel knew better. He knew that not every story was inconsequential. It seemed Jamie did too, because as soon as Curtis and Manchester were distracted, he leant forward and whispered,

'Do you really think the Mumford Boys will bite back?'

'I don't know,' Daniel replied. 'But we shouldn't take any chances.'

'How d'you mean?'

'I mean you shouldn't do your milk round for a while. None of us should go anywhere alone. We're safer as a group.'

'But what about my comics?' asked Jamie, his voice full of panic.

'You ever heard the expression 'an eye for an eye'?'

'Sure I have.'

'Well, if Marcus's eye really is busted, you'll find it pretty hard to read those comics when he catches you.'

Daniel gave him a serious nod, and Jamie slumped back in his chair.

'Shit, and I thought The Ogle was bad. I've never seen the Mumford Boys outside of school, and the first time I do, this happens.' He lifted his glass and took a swig of Coke, banging it back on the table like it was a hard whisky. 'Give me an Ogle any day...'

At that precise moment, the phone behind the bar started to ring. It was one of those old phones, the ones with a rotor, and it was loud. So loud it cut Curtis and Manchester off mid-conversation, which was quite the feat. Sam answered it. He squeezed the receiver into his shoulder so he could continue polishing glasses but gave up when it fell into the sink.

'Hello! Sorry!' He grabbed the phone in both hands. 'The Black Fox here, can I help you?'

There was a pause. Sam nodded and his eyes locked onto Daniel's.

'Of course, I'll pass you over to him.' He pulled the phone from his ear and beckoned Daniel over. 'It's for you...'

Daniel glanced at his friends, all of whom seemed to be just as shocked as he was. Even under the table, he could hear that Buster had stopped licking himself. No one was supposed to know they were there. So who was calling for him?

Quite slowly, he stood up, approached the bar, and took the phone from Sam.

'Hello...?' he said nervously.

To his surprise, it was his mother who greeted him. 'Peter?'

'Mum?'

'Daniel? What on Earth are you doing there?'

'You knew I was here. You rang for me.'

'I asked for your father.'

'Oh.'

Although Daniel knew it was his mum talking to him, she didn't quite sound like herself. It was as if there was something in her throat trying to keep her words from coming out. Like they were being churned through a grinder.

'You need to come home,' she said, further emphasising the peculiarity.

'I can't come home right now. We're —'

'Daniel. You need to come home.'

His mother was crying, weeping uncontrollably into the mouthpiece.

'What's wrong?' Daniel asked.

'It's your sister, Daniel. It's Daria. She's gone. She's gone and I can't find her. It's my fault —'

Daniel's mum broke off, crumbling into a fit of sobs, and Daniel's world turned white for a moment. The words, 'she's gone,' churned from one side of his head to the other, trying to turn into something solid. Something that made sense. But they couldn't, they couldn't, they couldn't. Until they could. The last echo ringed, and Daniel's vision returned. He glanced up at Sam, then at the painting behind him. The one with the white-eyed man. He could see the title now. The label underneath it was clear, and for the first time, Daniel realised what he was looking at.

MY VISION OF THE OGLE

by

Terry Bantam

And the eyes that had already been staring, stared all the harder. Like they knew him and knew him well. Every inch of him. From the scruff of his hair to the nook of his thumb.

THE AFTERNOON, 18 JUNE 2073

Three rays of light sliced through the blinds, casting thin gashes across the stranger's face. He remained in exactly the same position as half an hour ago. His posture hadn't changed. Only his eyes had displayed a slideshow of emotions. Happiness, anger, excitement, shock. Daniel's story was beginning to tick in his head, he could tell, and he wanted more. *Had* to have more. Even as the sun rose and the gashes stretched, and more of his face was taken over, all he cared about was the story. And for some reason, that made Daniel glad.

'Who was the last person to see her?' the stranger pondered, almost to himself.

'My mother,' Daniel replied.

'She said it was her fault.'

'Yes.' Daniel paused, picking slightly at some rough skin on his forearm. It came off quickly, ever the old husk that he was, and a bead of blood appeared in its place. He swallowed as he looked at it. 'She never left Daria in this house alone. But that morning, she'd gone to see Rupert. She'd left her handbag there the night before, and she wanted to pick it up. It was only supposed to be a sweeping visit.'

The stranger nodded and the rays of light rippled a little. 'How long was she gone?' he asked.

Daniel shrugged. 'She said around an hour.'

The stranger's eyes narrowed, and Daniel spotted a new emotion dancing in the middle of them.

'Fascinating,' he murmured. 'And she loved her daughter?'

'Of course she did,' Daniel replied.

He could sense some defensiveness in his voice, only he didn't quite know why it was there. It was his mother's fault; there was no doubt about that. He knew it. The stranger knew it. And yet a part of him still wanted to defend her. Perhaps that was the part he simply couldn't control. That inexplicable thing made of love and devotion, whispered by every mother into the heart of their child, and echoed back without question.

'She made a mistake,' Daniel said, clearing his throat. 'She got careless. And that's something no mother should ever do.'

'Did you hate her for what happened?'

'No,' said Daniel honestly. 'Hatred is an emotion rooted in surprise, but I wasn't surprised. A part of me knew. It fit my story. Besides, I had other emotions to deal with.'

'Such as?'

'Fear. I knew what had happened as soon as I put that phone down. Some things are written in ink, and I felt Daria's end was one of those things. Except...'

He trailed off, only it seemed the stranger knew where he was going. Like a reader greatly in tune with a book, he could predict what was going to happen next, even before he had turned the page.

'Except it wasn't written in ink,' he finished for him.

'Of course not,' Daniel replied. 'You know by now that this story is far stranger than that.'

Chapter Seven

WRITTEN IN BLOOD

The ground felt heavy beneath Daniel's feet. Ever since the fishing hole, everything around him had gathered weight. The ground felt heavy. The sky felt heavy. Even the air felt thick in his throat. It was the least he could do to hold his nerve and keep walking, but that's exactly what he had to do, because people were watching. Mrs Porter, Mr Arnold, the Capachi couple. All of them were walking in a sweep line across Bainden Field, glancing as often as they could at Daniel and his friends.

This was the first search of the day (there had already been two conducted the day before, in Ditchling Wood and near the old mill on Ringmere Farm), and Daniel knew it was pointless. The tip-off had come from Mrs Pippins, a decrepit seventy-year-old, who lived in an equally decrepit bedsit near the village primary school. She said she'd seen Daria on Sunday morning, eating some sweets and heading for Bainden Field. Indeed, the first thing they'd found was an empty packet of

Haribo tucked beside a utility pole. But Daria was a vocal opponent of Haribo. She hated them. And so the thought she'd been walking alone on a Sunday morning, munching away on a pack of sweets that she didn't even like (while also being around two inches too tall and wearing pink tights she didn't own) seemed unlikely.

Yet still, the search continued. Because the search had to continue. Only Daniel knew most of the searchers were just there for him. They wanted to gaze upon his face and watch his innocence drain in real time, and if that wasn't possible, they wanted to see his mother and offer their disapproving tuts and glares. None of them were there for the right reasons, and if they were, they were stupid. Because there was only one thing that had could have happened to Daria. And the culprit wasn't anywhere near Bainden field.

Daniel had told his friends as such on the day Daria disappeared:

'It's The Ogle. I know it is.'

'How do you know?'

'I can feel it. In my gut, I can feel it. We woke the beast. We angered it. And now it's come for me.'

'Why you? Why not any of us?'

But Daniel hadn't been able to answer that. He'd been trying to, because his dad had always told him to trust his gut. But the harder he thought about it, the further away an answer seemed to be.

As he thought about it now, the line moved further ahead. When Jamie, Curtis, and Manchester noticed he'd stopped, they lingered too. They were supposed to be five feet apart, but it didn't take long before gravity pushed the four of them together. By that point, the searchers were several yards in front of them, their attention pulled off Daniel and onto his mum, who led the pack from the front. And so the four of them could talk.

'Man, talk about rough,' said Curtis, shaking his head. 'It's not like you have shit on your face.'

'He doesn't,' said Manchester. 'I checked.'

Jamie prodded his trekking pole aimlessly into the grass. 'You okay, Dan?'

'Mmhm,' Daniel replied. Although really, he was trying to hold back tears for the fifth time that day.

Curtis smiled at him. 'Hey, look on the bright side. At least they're here. I mean, the whole village is out looking for Daria, even during teatime.'

'That's true.' Manchester nodded. 'I walked past the tearoom on my way here, and it was completely empty. Well, not completely empty. Mrs Pickens was still in there. But she's always in there. Maybe she lives there or something.'

'She does live there,' said Curtis. 'She's the owner, you muppet.'

'Well, excuse me if I'm not up to date on all the tearoom facts. I haven't been in there before, remember? Not everyone is as posh as you.'

'You went in there the other day to buy a gingerbread man.'

'Yeah, and it was shit.'

'Guys,' Jamie spoke up, clearly worried they might break into a wrestling match right in the middle of Bainden Field. 'We're getting a little off topic.'

Manchester and Curtis squared off for a few seconds. Then they looked at Daniel and thought better of it. Curtis patted him on the shoulder.

'I'm right, though. At least they're helping.'

'They're not helping. None of this is helping. Not unless we change these poles to pitchforks and march on Baltic Green, we won't get my sister back.'

'You really think it took her?' asked Jamie.

Daniel didn't have to say anything. His look alone told his friends it wasn't a good time to question his theory. Or, at least, it did for Curtis and Jamie.

'I dunno,' said Manchester, 'it seems a little far-fetched to me.'

With his free hand, he slipped out a pack of fruit pastilles, popping two of them onto his tongue. The bandages on his neck stretched and crinkled. He'd bought them from the corner shop two days ago, telling his mum he'd fallen off his bike.

'Hasn't your gut ever told you to do something?' asked Daniel.

'Yeah,' said Manchester. 'Mostly to eat.'

'And you listen to it?'

Manchester shrugged. 'When I'm hungry.'

'I'm talking about intuition. I don't know why The Ogle chose me out of all of us, I just know that it did.'

Curtis and Jamie stared at him unsurely. Manchester munched loudly on his fruit pastilles. Ahead of them, the line reached the opening of a copse and stopped, considering whether to move forward. Daniel took a deep breath.

'Listen,' he said quietly. 'One night, not long after we went to The Ogle House for the first time, I think I saw it.'

'You saw The Ogle?' Jamie gasped.

'Its shadow, yes. I was telling Daria a goodnight story, and when I went to leave, I saw a shadow on the other side of the door. Just for a second.'

'Maybe it was your mum.' Manchester spoke through another mouthful of pastels.

'She was downstairs,' Daniel replied through gritted teeth.

'Maybe it was your dog.'

'I don't have a dog.'

'You really should.'

Daniel scratched his thumb irritably. Since it was hot and he hadn't had a shower in at least three days, his cut had become more irksome, itching and throbbing any time he started to sweat. He scratched until it started to bleed.

'I know you guys find it hard to believe,' he murmured. 'I do too. A little. But ever since we went to that house, The Ogle has been watching me. It's been close. I know it.'

'Your thumb...' Jamie said then.

'What about it?'

'It's bleeding.'

'Yeah. So?'

Jamie's eyes were plastered on Daniel's hand, watching as the blood dripped onto the grass.

'It was bleeding at The Ogle House too.'

Manchester laughed. 'No shit, dickwad. That's where he cut it.'

'That's where *you* cut it,' Curtis corrected him. 'You hit the ball, remember?'

'And a fine shot it was too.'

'I mean your blood was there.' Jamie ignored them. 'On the porch. That's how I knew it was empty. That's why we went back. It was there the second time we went to The Ogle House too. I saw it.'

'Me too,' Daniel muttered.

'When we left, we thought we left without a trace, but maybe we didn't. Maybe we did leave something behind.'

Ahead of them, the group decided against the woodland and began making their way back towards them. Several faces renewed their examination of Daniel, but not his mother. Her eyes were on the ground. Her face pale and gaunt.

Curtis stared at Jamie, taking it all in. 'Are you saying The Ogle knew the blood belonged to Daniel?'

'Of all the stories we've heard about The Ogle, yeah, that doesn't seem too absurd.'

'But if The Ogle knew Daniel had been there, why did he take Daria?'

'Maybe he wants us to go back. Maybe she's bait.'

'He's right,' Daniel said suddenly. His words landed with such a weight, it was like his confidence reverberated through all of them. In that moment, they all believed the same thing. Their guts were aligned.

Manchester wavered a little. 'Shit...'

'But we can't go back,' said Curtis. 'We have no idea what we're dealing with.'

The murmurs of the crowd grew louder. The searchers were nearly back with them, so Daniel looked at his friends and whispered quickly,

'No. But we can find out.'

The Black Fox was heaving with punters. While the overcast skies had offered a brief respite two days ago, the sun was back to sizzling, making even the most hardened men lurk in dark corners and sip on their beers like it was water in a desert. In true British fashion, pessimism always seemed to negate reality, and so there wasn't any air con. At the very least, the windows were open, but without any breeze to speak of, this only gave the insects easy access. The bar was swarming with at least two dozen wasps and horseflies, hovering above every glass and taking the first bite of any food that came through the kitchen portal. Daniel swatted one away, wondering how something as sickly as beer could be worth this.

'Looks like not everyone got the message, Curtis.'

Jamie, Manchester, and Curtis were waiting in line behind him, their backs against the bar and their sweaty shirts beginning to leave damp stains on the wood. Jamie was smiling at Curtis wryly.

'You don't know that,' Curtis replied. 'Maybe it's their lunch break.'

'Organised searches don't tend to have lunch breaks. They're not on a rota.'

'Maybe they're just listening to their guts,' said Manchester.

He glanced at Daniel, checking to see if his remark had any teeth, but Daniel was too preoccupied to take notice. There were only two bartenders on service today. Sam, and another female Kiwi, who was far prettier than Sam. Daniel often enjoyed staring at her when he was here with his dad and Daria, but for the first time, he hoped the line fell in Sam's favour. He had no time for pretty blue eyes and curly dark hair right now.

Thankfully, the bar was in an 'L' shape, and more punters were gathering around the corner, so even though Daniel was the brunette's next customer, she decided to see to them instead. Either that, or he smelled.

'Hey, little Ottoman!' Sam called over when he spotted him. 'I heard about your sister, mate. It's awful. Send your dad my regards.'

Daniel and his friends moved up the bar until they were in front of Sam. The painting of The Ogle glared down at them.

'I will, thanks,' he said. Then he hesitated, wondering how best to open the conversation. He decided to just dive straight in. 'Hey, Sam, I'm wondering if you could tell me about the painting behind you.'

Sam glanced at it. 'Oh, yeah. Kind of creepy, isn't it? I don't know, I guess the owner liked it.'

'The owner of The Black Fox you mean?'

'Yeah, he collects artwork. The more local the better. I think they're for sale if you want.'

'No, thanks. I just wanted to know more about the artist.'

Sam checked the painting again. 'Terry? Interesting person. Hey, can I get you boys some Cokes?'

He was growing impatient, and although they hadn't said anything, Daniel could tell the punters behind them were too. He had to be quick.

'How d'you mean interesting?'

'Oh, I dunno. We didn't have a conversation. Hair was cool, though. Long and blue. Kind of whack.'

'Come on, mate,' said one of the punters. 'We're gasping here!'

Daniel turned to see a large man with huge, patchy sweat stains underneath his armpits. *Suck on them*, he thought. *It'll taste just the same.*

'Look,' said Manchester. 'Can you just tell us where Terry lives?'

'I'm sorry.' Sam shook his head. 'I can't give out addresses. Especially not for rugrats.'

'We're not going to do anything, we just want to know where —'

'Fledgling Street,' the sweaty punter interrupted. 'St Martha's House. My daughter volunteers there. Now would you please step aside so I can get some service?'

Without waiting for an answer, he barged into the four of them and slammed an empty glass down onto the bar. At any other time, Daniel might have taken issue with that — Manchester definitely would've — but to their surprise, the fat man had actually been their salvation. They left without saying another word, the white eyes of The Ogle watching them as they went.

The four of them had visited Fledgling Street once before, just last summer. It was close to Jamie's house in Hallows Down, and it was the steepest road in the village that didn't gather much traffic. It was the day after Manchester's birthday, and one of his presents had been a new skateboard. None of them knew how to skate, but they'd had a lot of fun sitting on their arses, feet flat on the nose, riding it down the road as fast as they could. It all ended with Manchester crashing into a parked Jaguar, which resulted in an angry letter to his parents and the confiscation of the skateboard in question. This was something Manchester quickly alluded to when they reached the top.

'I hope that Jaguar's still here. Think I'll bust the window this time.'

'Don't you think the dent was enough?' asked Curtis.

'Bastard robbed me of my skateboard. I think it's only fair I rob him of his car.' He slammed his fist into his palm. 'I'll beat it up so good, it'll be like driving a pencil case.'

'I seem to remember the car beating you up last time. How does it feel being the only person in history to get run over by a parked car?'

'How does it feel being the world's biggest bellend?'

'Guys, hold on.' Daniel put his hand up. He was staring at the bottom of the road, where a collection of searchers were rounding a corner. 'Here, behind the red box!'

Beckoning his friends towards him, Daniel ran onto the pavement towards an old, battered telephone box. The four of them gathered behind it as if standing in line for a phone call. As the searchers got closer, Daniel spotted his dad. Like his mum, he was at the head of the pack, talking to a couple of police officers. He looked tired. Almost haggard. Daniel's father was often unkempt, but this was something different. He walked like it wasn't just his clothes that were creased, but his whole body. The sight depressed him so much, he found himself fighting back tears again.

'Your dad's looking a little worse for wear,' Curtis whispered.

'What do you think he's gonna look like?' Daniel snapped.

'Sorry...'

'What do the police want with him?' asked Jamie.

Daniel shook his head. 'I don't know. They've been talking to both my parents. They even searched my house. My dad's house too.'

'This is crazy,' whispered Manchester.

The searchers reached the top of the road. Daniel's father disappeared from his view, and so he retreated from cover, rubbing his eyes. Once he was confident they were dry, he turned back to his friends.

'Okay, let's go. St Martha's House should be around here somewhere.'

'You know,' said Manchester, 'I'm not sure it is. The last time we were here, I don't recall seeing any house with that name on it.'

'Huh,' said Jamie. 'So it wouldn't be that one there with the sign saying, 'St Martha's House'?'

They followed his finger to a sign on the other side of the road, positioned outside a large, white property.

Manchester squinted at it. 'Hey, what d'ya know? I guess it's difficult to read when you're travelling at one hundred miles per hour.'

Jamie hummed in agreement. 'Knowing how to read in the first place would help too, I imagine.'

Daniel crossed the street and approached the front gate. He could hear muffled screaming. That in itself wouldn't have been cause for alarm, but the screams weren't normal. Normal screaming would be the cry of a baby, or the sound adults made when they were angry at each other. His mum and dad had done their share of normal screaming before they'd broken up. But these screams sounded juvenile. Not young, but not especially old either. The voice was breaking, so it probably belonged to a teenager, and there was no rhythm to it. No words. They were wild screams, incoherent, and followed every few seconds with a loud banging noise. When Daniel's friends caught up, they heard it too.

'What the hell is that?' Manchester asked.

The house had three floors (one more than any other property on this street), a pretty slate roof, and one of the rooms had dinosaur curtains in the window. To the left, Daniel could see a passageway leading to the back garden. On the other side of that garden was Argos Farm, and beyond that, Hallows Down, so he guessed they had a place to run if things went wrong. Reassured by that thought, Daniel lifted the hatch on the gate and made for the front door.

'I hope you're not thinking of ringing that bell,' Curtis called out.

'Why not?' asked Daniel.

'Can you not hear the screams? We should take a look first.'

The screaming broke, then grew more intense. It tumbled from one side of the house to the other, like the culprit was dashing through different rooms. The four of them reached the front door, and at the same moment, it flew open, shoving them to the ground like a line of dominoes.

As Daniel had suspected, a teenage boy was the culprit. He was a large boy, with dark skin, bulbous eyes, and a round, drooping belly. He glared at them like they were four aliens that had just dropped from the sky.

'MRS GUNN!' he shouted maniacally. 'INTRUDERS, MRS GUNN! INTRUDERS!'

A middle-aged woman, grey hair, grey skin, appeared from behind him. 'George! Come back inside! You're not allowed out by yourself!'

'BUT INTRUDERS, MRS GUNN! INTRUDERS!'

The woman called Mrs Gunn peered over George's shoulder, staring at Daniel and his friends as they climbed to their feet.

'Yes?' she said suspiciously. 'What do you want?'

Behind her, two more children appeared in the hallway. One, a girl about George's age, with chapped lips and crooked teeth. The other, younger than both, with what looked to be mustard in her hair.

'Uhh,' Daniel stuttered. 'We were just — we just wanted to know if —'

'THEY WANT TO ROB YOU!' screamed George. 'THEY'RE SWIPERS!'

'No, I swear we're not — '

'THEY'RE SWIPERS, MRS GUNN!' George stamped his feet and pointed at Daniel threateningly. 'NO SWIPING!'

Mrs Gunn grabbed him and turned him around. 'George, look at me. I'll deal with our visitors. In the meantime, maybe you can go get your dinosaurs to show them. Does that sound like something you can do?'

All of a sudden, George appeared to relax. His shoulders drooped, and when he spoke, his voice came out a lot softer.

'Why dinosaurs?'

'Because they might like your dinosaurs. Maybe they'll play with you.'

'PLAY!' George yelled, barging past Mrs Gunn and back into the house. 'PLAY! PLAY! PLAY!'

He bounded up the stairs at the end of the hallway, then Mrs Gunn stepped onto the porch and closed the door behind her, muffling the screams again.

'Do we really have to play with his dinosaurs?' whispered Manchester.

Despite all the screaming that clearly went on in this house, it appeared Mrs Gunn had good hearing.

'No,' she replied firmly. 'George has epilepsy and autism. It affects his short-term memory. He won't remember you in a few minutes.'

'So...' Curtis wavered. 'This is like a mental house?'

Mrs Gunn glared at him. 'It's a residential care facility.'

'Oh, yeah. That's what I meant.'

An awkward silence passed. *That might explain the painting*, Daniel thought. But even if that was the case, he was determined to find out more. Anything that could get him closer to saving his sister was something to follow up on, even if he was attacked for being a 'swiper' in the process.

'We're looking for someone,' he said. 'Terry Bantam. Is this the right place?'

'Are you friends?' asked Mrs Gunn.

'Yes. We met in The Black Fox, after the painting was delivered. We have a shared interest.'

Inside the house, George grew even louder. There seemed to be another kid involved, as the screams were accompanied by a girl yelling,

'THAT'S MY MUSTARD! GIVE IT BACK!'

Mrs Gunn let out a long, exhausted sigh. 'Okay, fine. It's best you don't come in the house, though. Not while George is like this. Terry's in the garden. You can get in around the side.'

She shooed the boys away and stepped back into the house, leaving Daniel, Curtis, Jamie, and Manchester standing there, wondering what they'd got themselves into.

'Jesus,' Manchester said after a few seconds. 'I dunno about you guys, but I'm not sure anyone in this loony bin is going to help us.'

'You shouldn't call it that,' Daniel replied.

He hopped down from the porch and made for the garden. The passageway to the side of the house was narrow and infested with nettles. This wouldn't have been a problem if the four of them had been wearing trousers. As it was, they were all in shorts, so by the time they made it through, their legs were covered in sores and throbbing in pain. Manchester hadn't even bothered to wear socks, so he got about a dozen more stings than the rest of them, but Daniel didn't have time to delight in it. His attention remained on his target. Terry Bantam.

He was sitting with his back to them at the end of the garden, his blue hair shining in the sun. A transparent tub of what looked like slugs was beside him. Daniel approached slowly. He knew he shouldn't be scared of a mentally challenged person, but he was also aware he'd never talked to one before. He had no idea how to do it. Stopping a good distance away from him, Daniel cleared his throat and made his presence known.

'Excuse me. We're looking for Terry Bantam. We were told he'd be here.'

The boy picked up another slug, then placed it delicately inside the tub. Daniel took a deep breath. *Just talk to him like you would talk to any other boy*, he thought. *It can't be that difficult.* But then the boy turned, and all of that went out of the window. Because Terry Bantam wasn't quite what they'd expected.

All of a sudden, Daniel and his friends found themselves staring into the large, brown eyes of a teenage girl. Light skinned. Full of freckles. And pretty.

'Seems you've been misinformed,' she answered playfully.

And if their palms hadn't been sweating in The Ogle House, or facing off against the Mumford Boys, they were certainly sweating now.

THE AFTERNOON, 18 JUNE 2073

Daniel took a last gulp of coffee and looked into the mug. Undissolved granules had settled into a paste at the bottom, and he knew why. He'd made this coffee in a rush, his legs shaking. But that had been a while ago, and as more of his story had been told, he'd steadily felt calmer. Inviting the stranger into his home had been scary, but now he was inside, everything felt strangely comfortable. The stranger was by the counter, his face warm and engaged. Junebug was now curled up on Daniel's lap, purring gently. Things were normal. And that felt good.

'Would you like a refill?' the stranger asked.

Daniel nodded. 'Please.'

'Would you mind if I had some more tea? I've never tried the Cornish stuff before. And you're right, it's perfect.'

'Of course.'

The stranger walked to the kitchen cabinets and began preparing their beverages. He'd clearly been watching Daniel as he'd done it, as he remembered where everything was.

'So,' he said, removing the sugar satchels from the drawer by the fridge, 'did you notice anything funny about Manchester?'

Daniel faltered slightly. 'Do you need me to tell this story? Seems you know it already.'

'I'm sorry. I tend to jump ahead.'

'No, I didn't notice anything funny. But it's fair to say my mind was elsewhere.'

'But when you look back, I mean.'

'Perhaps he seemed a little more stand-offish than usual. But he was usually pretty stand-offish. It wasn't the most jarring thing at St Martha's House.'

'And the girl…' The stranger flicked the kettle on, turning to him with a wry smile. 'You described her as pretty.'

'Did I?' mumbled Daniel nonchalantly.

'Yes, you did.'

'Maybe she was. But I wasn't concerned about that. I was looking for my sister.'

The stranger's smile stretched wider. 'I thought this was a true story.'

Daniel went to say something, but then he stopped himself. The stranger's smile was beginning to annoy him, so he looked out of the window to avoid it. The sun was still shining. The sky was clear and blue. Some might have said there was nothing bluer than a sky like this, but Daniel would know better. He knew Terry. Her freckles, her eyes, her hair. Looking at this sky brought him right back to that day in August, sixty-nine years ago, and that made him glad. Because in many ways, this story was a hard one to tell. There were shadows and scars, blood and monsters. There was death and bad things, and days that lived forever in his nightmares.

But there was also Terry. And her blue hair. And that made everything just a little bit sweeter.

Chapter Eight

BANTAM OF DEANSHIRE

Daniel noticed the bandages. They started at the palms of her hands and travelled the length of her forearms. There were doodles on both of them. Or not quite doodles. More miniature works of art, drawn with intricacy and care. On the left, there was an ocean, stark blue and frothing. On the right, there was a jungle. It wasn't quite as good as the left one (she was probably right-handed), but it was still good enough to draw Daniel's eyes away from her face for a few seconds, and that was quite the feat, because her face was beautiful. Not beautiful in the conventional sense. She wasn't as clearly pretty as Carol, who was pinned up in Curtis's treehouse, or as plainly attractive as the brunette in The Black Fox. But she was captivating. Her eyes were so dark, she didn't seem to have any pupils at all, and her face, though covered in freckles, seemed to glow in the sun.

She was wearing a loose-fitting top, and on her collarbone, there was a tattoo of a tiger. That took Daniel by surprise, because although the girl was clearly a teenager, she didn't seem that much older than him. As far as Daniel was aware, you weren't allowed to get a tattoo until you were at least in your twenties. Perhaps even older. He looked at his friends, all of whom were just as speechless as him. That didn't shock Daniel, either. None of them had really talked to a girl before. There had been moments here and there, like asking to borrow a pen in maths class, or saying 'yes' when a girl asked to have some gum. But that was about it. Some of the other kids at school had girlfriends, but Daniel had never been that successful. The closest he'd got to a genuine interaction with a girl was when he'd been asked to read out the class register one morning. He'd been in third-year, and he'd had a crush on a girl called Molly Sparrow for six months. He remembered the butterflies in his belly when he'd read out her name, and he remembered the way his heart had fluttered when she'd said back, 'Here'.

That had been the pinnacle of his success, but now he'd have to take things one step further. For the first time in his life, he'd have to initiate a conversation with a girl. And not just any girl, but a girl who was older than him, pretty, and had a tattoo to boot. He plucked up the courage and started talking.

'Hello, I'm...' Daniel caught himself, then gestured to his friends. 'We're Daniel...'

Terry frowned and Daniel felt his stomach sink. *You really are a sad, strange little boy*, he thought. In the corner of his eye, he saw Curtis facepalm.

'I mean, *I'm* Daniel. And these are my friends, Jamie, Manchester, and Curtis.'

The girl took them in, shielding her eyes from the sun. Then she said, 'Cute,' and turned back to the flower bed.

Daniel glanced at his friends, all of whom shrugged in unison. 'We wanted to ask you something. About the painting of yours hanging in The Black Fox.'

'Go ahead,' said Terry.

'Why did you paint it?'

The girl made a loud snorting sound, as if Daniel's question was highly amusing. 'Hey, Rousseau,' she laughed, 'why did you paint *The Dream*?'

Daniel blinked. He wasn't quite sure who Rousseau was, but he decided not to ask. Maybe it was some sort of crazy talk. He had to remember, while the girl was pretty, she could still be completely nuts. He gave a false laugh of his own.

'Yeah, well, I would really like to know. I think it might help me, you see.'

'Come here, little fella...' Terry snatched another slug from the flower bed, placing it inside the tub along with the others. 'There you go. Don't fight in there. I have no room for criminals.'

Daniel had suspicions on the word 'Rousseau', but now he was entirely sure. Like his sister, this girl had a lisp that made all of her 'S' sounds suffer. He didn't know if he believed in signs, but if they did exist, this would surely be a good one.

'Hey, Terry,' Manchester jumped in. 'We're kind of on a tight schedule. Life or death kind of thing, you know.'

Terry laughed again. 'Then you chose the wrong person to have a conversation with. I don't care about anyone's time but my own. By the way, you have a bogey.'

She hadn't even looked at him, but she must have been right, because Manchester was suddenly blowing his nose into his armpit, his face stark red.

'See,' said Terry, 'wasn't that kind of me?'

'Why are you called Terry anyway?' Manchester shot back at her. 'You do know that's a boy's name, right?'

'It was the only one that made sense, I'm afraid. My real name's Esther. A lisper's nightmare. There aren't many ways you can shorten it, so Terry had to do.'

Daniel felt they were getting a little side-tracked, so before Manchester could get in another jibe, he stood between them and put on another false smile.

'Anyway, can we get back to the painting? I just wanted to know —'

'FUCK OFF! FUCKING SHOVE IT! STUPID LITTLE KIDS! FUCK! OFF!'

The outburst came out of nowhere and nearly gave Daniel a heart attack. Terry screamed at them with pure venom. Then, as if nothing had happened, she swivelled back to the flower bed and renewed her search for slugs. Daniel swayed slightly. Behind him, Manchester, Jamie, and Curtis took several steps backwards, their hands raised like she might be about to attack.

'Come on, little sluggies,' said Terry happily. 'These flowers aren't for you. Come to Auntie Terry.'

'She's insane.' Manchester gawped at her, not even trying to keep his voice down. 'Absolutely insane.'

'No,' replied Terry. 'They have the pick of all the flowers in this garden. I just don't want them to eat these ones. They're sweet peas, and they're my favourites.' Terry grabbed another slug, one that had hidden itself under the crest of the plant, and she placed it in the tub. 'That should do. Don't want to overcrowd them. Now, you wanted to ask me about my painting?'

She turned back to Daniel with a wide smile, and for once in his life, he found himself agreeing with Manchester. This girl really was insane.

'Umm. Yeah, I did. I mean, I do.'

And then it happened again. All of a sudden, Terry's face changed, and her lips grew tight.

'FUCKING LITTLE TIME-WASTING PRICK!'

'Sorry,' Daniel said, holding his own hands up.

'Fuck! Shit! Wanker! Sort your hair out, mate. You're a fucking sheep!'

She swore again, but this time, Daniel noticed something different. Her voice was quieter. Shaking. But not angry. In fact, it didn't look like there was venom in her face at all. He'd misread it. Her face was in pain, almost twisted, like she was trying to stop the words from leaving her mouth. Her eyes were wide and apologetic. Terry jolted violently, then went back to normal again, and Daniel stood there, feeling about two heartbeats off a cardiac arrest.

'Sorry,' she said quietly. 'I don't mean to — Fucking little sheep boy with his booger friends!' She twitched and began humming. 'It's my tics. I have Tourette's.'

Daniel wavered. *Okay*, he thought. *She's not about to kill me. She has a thing. And the thing has a name. That's positive.*

'Umm,' he mumbled. 'What's Tourette's?'

'It's a thing I have that stops me being able to control myself. I say mean things, but I don't actually mean it.'

'Sounds like what Manchester has,' said Curtis.

'Fuck off,' said Manchester.

'See.'

Terry laughed. 'Normally I have a card that goes around my neck. But I didn't think I'd need one today, being at home and all.'

'Can Manchester get one of those?' asked Curtis. 'It could really help us out in some situations.'

'Sure thing, I have a spare.'

Daniel watched the girl's expression soften. As she did so, he found his heart rate returning to normal, the tension releasing somewhat. It was like she was casting a silent spell, enchanting them all into a false sense of security. But now he knew what to expect, Daniel resisted sinking all the way into it. When he spoke, he did so with his eyes creased, preparing for another onslaught.

'So, you live here, huh?'

This question had nothing to do with Daria or the painting, but for some reason, Terry herself had become more interesting to him. Perhaps it was the spell. Daniel tried harder to resist.

'No,' she replied bluntly. 'This is my holiday home. I live in a big mansion in Barbados — Fuck off, sheep boy! — and I travel down here to — FUCK! SHIT! I'M GONNA KILL YOU!'

She yelled and spat, but then she ended the sentence with the most pleasant-sounding whistle Daniel had ever heard in his life. He watched as she tapped herself rhythmically on the chest.

'That was gonna be a great joke, I swear.'

'You do,' said Manchester.

'Wanker. Ooh, strawberries. Strawberries in my hat, gonna fucking mash 'em!'

Daniel heard Curtis laugh behind him, and for a moment, he was worried it might make her even worse. But despite the discomfort Terry was in, she started chuckling too.

'It gets worse when I'm around strangers,' she explained.

She jolted and made a popping sound with her lips, and all of a sudden, Daniel felt very sorry for her. Terry was probably the prettiest girl he'd ever met. Even prettier than Molly Sparrow. And yet it was like her brain was against her, trying everything in its power to make her appear ugly. He watched her silently for a moment, thinking about what he could do to help.

'Maybe I should have been more specific,' he said after a few seconds. 'My name's Daniel Ottoman. This is Manchester Harbury, Jamie Watt, and Curtis Partridge-King. There, now we aren't strangers, see?'

Terry chuckled again. 'I'm cured...'

Daniel found himself standing a little taller. 'Okay, great. Can I ask you about the painting now?'

'You better had, before I tell you to fuck off again.'

Daniel hesitated, thinking carefully about how he should phrase this. 'I know why people paint. But I wanted to know about this painting in particular. Why did you paint The Ogle?'

'You're looking for it, huh?'

'Maybe,' Daniel replied. He thought it was better to be cryptic than to provide the whole truth. At least at this stage.

'I paint things that I see. It started as a way to communicate. To get people to see me better, without all the stuff that gets in the way. But after a while, I stopped caring about that. I realised art was far deeper than what people were capable of understanding. If anything, it just made them more confused, so I just did it for me. To help me understand what was going on beneath the surface.'

Daniel nodded, although he understood nothing of what she'd just said. He didn't study art at school, but if he did, it was probably another subject he would fail.

'The Ogle is more than just a monster,' Terry continued. 'It's deeper than that. It's worse.'

'You mean it's real?'

It was Jamie who asked this question, only Daniel wished he hadn't, because it seemed to confirm something Terry was thinking. With a little sigh, she grabbed her tub of slugs and stood up.

'Of course it's real,' she said bluntly. 'But like everyone else, it's not something you kids are gonna understand.'

Suddenly bored of the conversation, she breezed past them and headed towards the house, stopping only to tear some leaves from a seemingly less important plant.

'I'm not joining you in your little monster hunt,' she said, stuffing the leaves into her pocket. 'So you can say goodbye to that idea. It was nice to meet you, though. Sorry for swearing at you.'

'It has my sister!' Daniel called back. 'The Ogle. It has my sister.'

The crypticness hadn't lasted long, but it was the only thing Daniel could think to do to get Terry to stay. To his relief, she hesitated. Then, slowly, she turned back.

'Did you tell Mrs Gunn who you were?' she asked.

'Kind of,' Daniel replied.

'And she let you in here?'

'We said we were friends.'

A few seconds passed. Terry broke into another soft, delicate smile, brighter than the sun. She gestured the boys towards her.

'Follow me,' she said.

She slid open the French doors and disappeared into St Martha's House. But the boys lingered, none of them quite knowing what to do next.

'Do we follow her?' Jamie whispered.

'It's up to sheep boy,' Manchester replied.

And Daniel made his decision. Thinking only about his sister (and perhaps, to a lesser extent, the way that smile had lit up Terry's face), he marched towards St Martha's House, walked inside, and waited for his friends to follow him.

Terry had already reached the stairs by the time they'd all entered the kitchen. She put a finger to her lips, urging them to be quiet. In the other room, Daniel could hear children, around four of them in total, all of whom were talking over each other and playing a game of some sort. Directly above them, George was still screaming. His feet slammed against the floor, causing small clouds of dust to fall from the ceiling and land on Daniel's head. He brushed it off, then followed Terry quickly into the hallway and up the stairs. Before they could reach the top, they were met by another kid on the way down. This one was also female, though far less attractive than Terry. She had a pig-like nose, thick, bushy eyebrows, and it looked like she hadn't washed her hair in years.

'You're not allowed to bring visitors upstairs, Terry.'

'I'm fourteen years old,' Terry replied. 'I can do what I like.'

'And you're supposed to be hiding that tattoo. You know it was illegal to get that.'

'Oh, fuck off, Margaret.'

Margaret scowled at her, cheeks puffing. 'Mrs Gunn told you to work on your Tourette's.'

'That wasn't Tourette's. That was me. Fuck off.'

Terry barged past her and opened the first door on the landing. Daniel and his friends followed, and Jamie closed the door behind them, blocking a furious-looking Margaret out of sight.

Terry's bedroom was a mess. The bed was a tangle of sheets and clothes, and the floor was littered with paper scraps, empty juice cartons, and paintbrushes. In the corner, there was a stencil holding a half-finished painting of a garden. On the walls, lopsided pieces of art had been nailed clumsily into the plaster. The largest depicted a jungle and a fierce storm, with a scared-looking tiger hiding in some ferns. The room smelled funny too. It smelled like a boy's room, so it felt a little familiar. But that changed when Daniel spotted the radiator in front of the window, which was topped with a line of bras and knickers. It was only then that he remembered this was a girl's room. Not wanting to come across as a pervert, he averted his gaze from the underwear and looked at Terry, who was pulling a small fish tank from under the bed. Inside were more slugs, along with chunks of wood and some grass. She tipped the contents of the tub inside, as well as the leaves from her pocket.

'Here you go, little fellas. Welcome to Casa De Slug. Feeding time is at twelve-thirty every day, and new bedding is provided every Friday. Toilets are in the far-left corner, and please be aware, there's no smoking area. If you need to smoke, please trickle out slowly and make sure you're at least five feet away from the tank. You can then use our courier service to make your way back. That's me.' She raised a hand. 'Hello.'

Daniel, Manchester, Jamie, and Curtis stood there dazedly. All of them were probably thinking the same thing. Daniel had always assumed his first time in a proper girl's room would be an alien experience. He'd be surrounded by cleanliness and normal girl things, complete with a pristine makeup table and a glass cabinet full of sweet-smelling perfume. He'd imagined sparkling pink furniture and heavenly orchestral music, but it was clearly all a myth.

Terry turned back to them and noted their faces. 'Ah, sorry. I'll get the slug smell out.' She opened a window, and years of female idealisation went out with it.

'I like your paintings,' said Jamie awkwardly.

'Fuck off, nerdy birdy,' said Terry.

She closed her eyes and twitched a little, and Jamie stared down at his feet. He looked embarrassed, but Daniel could see where Terry was coming from. His glasses did give his eyes a beady look, and his nose was just about pointy enough to look like a beak. Over the years, they'd tried and failed to come up with some mean nicknames for Jamie, but that one hit the nail on the head immediately. Tourette's must have been terrible to live with, but it was certainly perceptive.

'Thank you.' Terry started over. 'They're Rousseau's. People don't seem to get him as an artist, but I do. Like this one...' She approached the painting of the storm and the tiger. 'It's called

Surprised!. Most people think this is an intense, visceral look at the fierceness of nature. But I think it goes deeper than that. Beneath the surface.'

She raised her finger, using it like a pointer, as if she was giving them a full-on presentation. 'There are three distinct parts to it. The tiger is us, the jungle is our mind, and the storm represents external influence. Everyone knows that the tiger is the king of the jungle, yes? But it's more than that. He's shaped by it. The jungle has made him king by forcing him to be the apex predator. Except the storm changes that, because the storm changes the jungle. Rousseau uses deliberate yet wild brushstrokes to invoke a sense of chaos, and that chaos makes the tiger weak and afraid, simply because he's being faced with something outside of his control. His world has been changed. The jungle created the tiger, sure, but what has the storm created? Disorder. Anxiety. And the result? Surprise!'

A moment passed. The boys stared at her dumbly, none of them quite knowing what to do with that information. Then Jamie spoke up again.

'I like your blinds too. Are they cotton?'

Terry blinked at him. 'So,' she said. 'You kids think The Ogle has taken someone.'

'Yes,' said Daniel, pleased to get back to the subject at hand. 'It's taken my sister, and I think you could help us.'

'How can I help you?'

'Because you created that painting, which means you've seen The Ogle. I think we have a better chance of getting my sister back if we know our enemy.'

On the other side of the house, George's stamping grew louder, to the point where it felt like the whole room was vibrating. Terry crossed her arms and ignored it, apparently all too familiar with the sensation.

'Why do you think The Ogle took your sister? Have you seen it?'

'No,' Daniel replied. 'But we went to The Ogle House.'

'Why?'

'Because we were bored,' said Manchester nonchalantly.

Terry raised an eyebrow. 'Do you often do stupid things when you're bored?'

'Do you often talk to slugs?'

'We went there because we were curious,' Daniel interjected, adamant they stay on track this time. 'I suppose curiosity got the better of us. But the point is, we made a mistake. We left something behind.' He raised his thumb, turning his hand around to reveal the long, red gash, which was still raw from where he had scratched it this morning. 'My blood...'

Terry hummed, then made that funny popping sound with her lips again. 'And then your sister goes missing, and you put two and two together? Doesn't seem like much to go on.'

'I'm going on my gut,' replied Daniel defensively.

'If your gut told you to look for The Ogle in the big, scary monster house, then I don't think it's the most reliable thing to listen to.'

The boys looked at each other, confused. Terry laughed, hopping on top of the windowsill.

'You mean,' said Jamie, 'The Ogle doesn't live there?'

'Oh, it lives there. But that's not where you're gonna find it.'

'Is this your Tourette's playing up again?' asked Manchester impatiently. 'Or are you just being deliberately illogical?'

'Did you not listen to my art lesson? Sometimes you have to look deeper. Beneath the surface. The Ogle isn't from our world; it's from somewhere else.'

The room was vibrating even harder now. George's stamps were becoming more violent. But all of them were completely still. Even Terry looked a little more rigid. If Daniel had known her better, he might even have said she looked frightened.

'How do you know this?' he asked timidly.

'Because I know The Ogle. I didn't just see it — Fuck off! Fuck off! Strawberries! Strawberries in a hat, mash 'em.' Terry stumbled on her words and made another perfect whistling sound. She recomposed herself and tried to continue. 'I saw it and I knew it, and those eyes — Fuck off! Fuck off! Shit! — It was like there was a connection I couldn't explain.' She twitched and fidgeted, then took a deep, shaky breath. 'You came to me for help, and you were right to. But not because of the painting, because of me. If you want to find it, I'm your best chance.'

There was a scream, a door slamming, and then the sound of George's footsteps reverberated on the landing. He marched downstairs, yelling happily about all the mustard he had in his hair. Someone chased after him.

'Okay,' said Curtis, 'but do we really wanna find it? Now we know for sure it exists. I mean, we thought he could have taken Daniel's sister as bait. You know, to lure us back in.'

'Because you're so special...'

Daniel felt a tinge of embarrassment bite into his chest. He couldn't see it, but he was sure he was blushing.

'Well,' said Manchester, 'it's not like you're so special either. Are you seriously telling us you know so much about The Ogle because you looked into its eyes? I look into Buster's eyes everyday, but I don't know what he's thinking when he's taking a shit.'

Jamie let out a nervous laugh. Curtis did too. Terry, however, looked more serious than ever. Her dark eyes narrowed, and she jumped off the windowsill, deciding instead to pace the room slowly. She was fiddling a little with her bandages, pulling the slip out of position, then back into the crease between her thumb and forefinger.

'I looked into its eyes, yes. I was six years old, and it came to me.'

'But that's how old my sister is,' said Daniel. 'That's Daria's age.'

The knot in his chest was twisting into something different now. The embarrassment had eked away, and he was left with nothing but anticipation, such anticipation that he could feel it in his throat. Terry walked back to the painting on the wall and stopped directly below the tiger. She turned, and Daniel realised he didn't have to know her better. What had been hiding beneath the surface was now written all over her face. Terry Bantam was frightened.

'What a coincidence,' she replied briskly. 'That's when it took me too.'

THE AFTERNOON, 18 JUNE 2073

'Did you like her?'

The stranger was sitting opposite Daniel now, stroking the rim of his mug. That curious smile was back on his face.

Daniel shook his head disbelievingly. 'I just told you this girl was kidnapped by The Ogle, at the exact same age as my sister, and you're concerned about whether or not I liked her. You're worse than the British tabloids.'

The stranger reclined in his chair. 'Tell me, does the fact her hair was blue play any significance in this story?'

'No.'

'And yet you mentioned it at least three times. And her eyes.'

A moment passed. Daniel's face hadn't flushed for a long time, perhaps not since he was a kid, but he could feel himself flushing now.

'I guess I'm just perceptive,' he said unconvincingly.

'Interesting,' the stranger replied. 'I still don't know what Curtis's hair colour was. Or Jamie's.'

Daniel's face flushed harder, and he let out a slight sigh. He supposed it was foolish trying to hide it. His feelings for Terry were as plain then as they were now, and while he could say that he'd grown, and aged, and lived long enough to bury his emotions, so long as there was blood left in him to blush, his body would always betray him.

'Fine,' he said. 'I liked her. She was a teenage girl, and I was eleven years old. Of course I liked her. It was a scientific certainty. The only one that made sense.'

'Did you trust her?'

The question came out of nowhere, but the stranger had asked it quite earnestly, as he was now staring intently at Daniel, the smile completely vanished from his face.

'Did you?' he repeated when Daniel didn't answer.

'Brown and blonde. That was their hair colour.'

'Excellent. I feel like I know them better already. Did you know Terry?'

Daniel cleared his throat. 'I had no reason not to trust her.'

The stranger's face went soft again, and he went back to stroking his mug. Daniel watched him coldly. Telling a story to someone who already knew so many parts of it was exhausting. But he knew he had to go on. There was strength in going on, and Daniel had always been strong. That was something else that hadn't changed.

Outside, a gust of sea wind rippled through the garden, causing the sweet peas to tap, tap, tap, against the kitchen window. They fell into the rhythm of the story.

Chapter Nine

THE THORNE THEORY

'The Ogle took you?'

Terry stood beneath the tiger, staring back at Daniel with large, tear-filled eyes. He'd told Daria a lot of stories in his time, with a heap of different characters. But looking at Terry Bantam, not one of them had the kind of backstory she had. There was a whole world inside those eyes. Lived, suffered, and kept secret.

'Yes,' she said quietly. 'The Ogle took me. Just like it's taken your sister.'

Daniel frowned. If he was a little older, he may have been able to make it out. But for now, her lips moved, but her eyes remained silent.

'You're alive, though,' said Jamie.

Terry glanced at him. 'Those glasses are coming in handy.'

'But how can you be alive if The Ogle took you?' asked Daniel.

'I guess I had good parents. I was just six years old when I was taken, and I don't remember much of it. It was almost like I was dreaming. I was lying in bed — Fuck! Shit! Drama queen! — and The Ogle was standing over me, staring into my eyes.'

She patted her chest and gave another whistle, and Daniel thought back to that painting in The Black Fox. He thought about its eyes. Those hideous, white eyes, devoid of humanity. The Ogle hadn't been depicted as a monster in that painting. In many ways, it looked more human than Daniel ever would have imagined, but that somehow made it worse. It was one of them. Only it was wrong. Blank and lifeless. A void in human clothes, like a black hole disguised as the sun. He couldn't imagine what it would be like to see something like that in the flesh. But that's exactly what his sister was seeing. Right now. And the very thought made him sick.

'I was lost,' Terry continued. 'Lost, cold, and afraid. In a world of darkness. With just one thing in the centre. A blue spiral. Like one of those windows you see on ships, only it was moving.'

'Like a portal?' Jamie asked.

'Maybe.'

'How'd you mean you *had* good parents?' Daniel questioned.

Terry started swearing again. A jumble of 'shits' and 'fucks', and, for some reason, 'strawberries', blurred her speech.

'I'm not sure how long it had me,' she said, rubbing her chest. 'In some ways, it felt like I was staring at that spiral forever. But then my parents were staring back at me. Like they were in the middle of it, reaching down. The next thing I knew, I was awake and alive. And they were gone.'

Daniel swallowed. His parents would never believe that The Ogle had taken Daria, he was quite sure about that. But either way, he didn't want to risk losing them. If Terry's parents hadn't come back, why would his story be any different?

'I don't want my parents to save her,' he said, almost to himself.

'I concur,' said Terry. 'But that does put us in a bit of a pickle.'

'There's no pickle. I'll do it. I've been to The Ogle House before and came away alive. I can do it again.'

'Have you not been listening? I told you, you're not gonna find The Ogle in that house.'

'So where are we gonna find it?' asked Manchester impatiently.

Terry glared at him. In a flash, the tears in her eyes disappeared. She pushed herself away from the painting and placed her hands behind her back.

'Let me ask you something. Have you ever had something you shouldn't have? A cigarette? A dirty magazine? A pack of condoms?'

Daniel felt his cheeks go warm and he looked down at his feet. Terry smiled naughtily.

'Okay, maybe you're not quite there yet. But you do know what I mean, right? Something bad that you don't want your parents to see. Where do you hide it?'

She stopped in front of Curtis, waiting for an answer.

'Under my bed?' he said awkwardly.

Terry nodded and turned to Jamie.

'Under my bed,' he agreed.

Then she turned to Daniel.

'Under the bed,' he said quietly.

Terry turned and approached her own bed, pushing the tank of slugs back underneath with her foot. 'Me too,' she said.

Manchester shrugged. 'So what? The Ogle has hidden Daria under its bed?'

'Its bed. Its home. Its refuge. Like I said, The Ogle isn't from our world. It's from somewhere else.'

'Okay,' said Manchester. 'So where is it?'

'I don't know.'

'You said it took you.'

'I was six.'

There was a pause. Daniel glared at Manchester, trying to understand what he was getting at. Terry remained perfectly calm. She was standing in front of the window now, her hands still behind her back.

'All I remember is the blue spiral,' she continued. 'And my parents. I remember them.'

'Okay, great,' Manchester replied sarcastically. 'Well, it was lovely to meet you.'

'And you, boogerman.'

'No,' said Daniel. 'We can't leave. We need to think about this.'

'Think about what?' said Manchester. 'She hasn't given us anything.'

'She's told us there's a portal to another dimension right here in Deanshire. I think that's something.'

With a laugh that was totally devoid of humour, Manchester walked up to Jamie and patted him on the shoulder.

'Hey, Jamie. Have you spotted any portals on your milk round? No? Okay then.'

'It's not like he was looking.'

Jamie raised his hand. 'To be fair, I think that's something I'd notice.'

'Maybe we can ask Champ the Tramp,' suggested Curtis. 'He's been around.'

Manchester laughed again. 'Oh, good idea, Curtis. Let's ask the mad tramp who's on his fifth whisky of the day whether he's seen any strange portals floating about.'

'Well, what do you wanna do?' Daniel shot back at Manchester. 'You just wanna let my sister die?'

'I just think we need more to go on,' said Manchester. 'And I think there's a reason she can't give it to us.'

Terry was standing in the same position, silently watching them. The left side of her mouth was curled slightly.

'She's told us everything she knows,' said Daniel confidently.

'Has she?'

'ESTHER!'

Mrs Gunn's voice echoed from downstairs, causing all of them to jump and turn towards the door. All of them but Terry, who let out a loud, bored-sounding sigh.

'That's me tattled on. I thought it was taking a while.'

'Wait!' Daniel raised his hands. 'Don't go.'

'Look, this has all been very cute, but I don't appreciate being called a liar. Especially not by the boogerman over here — Fuck! Shit! Wanker!'

'He's sorry,' Daniel pleaded.

'No, I'm not,' said Manchester.

'Then *I'm* sorry. Look, I —'

'I've told you everything I know.' Terry cut over him. 'Now it's up to you to put your heads together. You can meet me tomorrow with what you have. I'll be at Eastdow Meadows at nine o'clock, near the swing set. In the meantime, I suggest you leave out the window. You won't be seen, and I can get away with calling Margaret a big fat liar. Don't worry, it's not a big drop.'

And with that, she was gone, leaving the four of them standing alone in her bedroom. They listened to her footsteps bounding quickly down the stairs. Curtis scratched his head.

'Did she just give us an assignment?'

Jamie nodded slowly. 'It did sound a bit like that.'

'Thanks a lot, Manchester,' hissed Daniel.

'It's not my fault I don't trust her. People like that just want attention.'

'How would you know?'

'Because I know the type. And unlike you losers, I'm not blindsided by the fact she's a girl.'

'I don't care about that,' Daniel said defensively.

'Oh please, you've been drooling more than my dog.'

'I care about my sister.'

Manchester laughed. 'If you care about your sister, maybe you should look for her, and not spend your time lusting after some blue-haired freak. Just a suggestion.'

Despite being so against Terry, he proceeded to take her advice. Striding across the bedroom, he opened the window and peered down towards the terrace. Daniel did too. The drop was indeed minimal. The biggest danger was twisting an ankle on impact, but they'd all jumped out of trees numerous times, and none of them had failed to stick a landing just yet. Manchester hooked one leg across the sill.

'Oh, and she's got a boyfriend anyway. Didn't you see the picture on her bedside table? Or were you too busy drooling?'

Before Daniel could answer, Manchester dropped from the window and landed with a grunt on the terrace. To his disappointment (but not to his surprise), there wasn't a great crack or a scream of pain. Instead, Manchester got to his feet, dusted himself down, and ran quickly towards the road. Curtis was next. Then Jamie. Before Daniel followed them, however, he took a peek at the bedside table in question. Just as Manchester had noted, a small, framed photograph rested on top, propped beside a collection of flower bracelets and empty crisp packets.

It showed Terry with that familiar blue hair, standing beside a boy of similar age, with a light patch of stubble lining his upper lip. They were arm in arm, laughing, and standing in the middle of a field with green crops on either side of them. In their hands, they were lifting what looked like two large strawberries to the camera, but Daniel didn't have time for a closer inspection. A few seconds later, he heard the sound of footsteps on the stairs again, and fearing the wrath of Mrs Gunn (or the even more dangerous wrath of George), he climbed onto the window, took a deep breath, and dropped down to the ground. He landed perfectly on his feet and then raced after his friends.

Much of the rest of the day was spent in deep conversation. The boys walked back to the high street, collected a few sodas from the corner shop (two Cokes for Daniel and Jamie, a Tizer for Manchester, and a cream soda for Curtis), then made their way to the tennis courts on Eastdow Meadows, where they discussed everything Terry had told them.

Despite knowing that they'd never seen a magic portal lingering around Deanshire, they talked intently about where it could be and where they could rule out. The Black Fox didn't seem likely. Daniel had been there plenty of times with his dad, and the only thing out of the ordinary was the owner's glass eye — which, come to think of it, could have been the reason he liked those modern art pieces so much. The tearoom was also a certain no. Being a sanctuary of gossip, it was almost impossible that none of the upper-class, snooty clientele would mention it over their sandwiches and tea.

'Oh, yes, I for one am shocked about Mildred's secret love affair. Almost as shocked as that time I found a magic portal in the utility cupboard by the bathroom. Do you remember? I opened the wrong door.'

In fact, nowhere in Deanshire seemed likely. Between them, they'd already explored every nook and cranny it had to offer, and there was nothing to suggest it was anything other than the boring country village it appeared to be.

Manchester spent most of the conversation pacing around the courts and kicking the weeds, his hands buried in his pockets and an ugly scowl plastered across his face. The only time he ever spoke was to reiterate how much of a nut Terry was, and how they should all put their attention on something else. But he wasn't very successful.

Then again, neither were the rest of them. After three hours of debate, none of them had landed on anything of value, and it had also grown a lot colder. The sky above them had filled with mean-looking clouds, threatening to burst at any moment, and so they each decided to pack it in for the day and do some solitary thinking. They would reconvene by the swing set, just as Terry had said, and hopefully, by then, one of them would have had a bright idea.

The clouds opened on Daniel's way home. By the time he reached his doorstep, he was soaked from head to toe, his shoes squelching and his nose filled with that smell of dust that always came whenever the rain spoiled a sunny day. He'd hoped to slip into the house as quietly as he could, but all subtlety was lost when a flash of lightning heralded the door's opening, and a thick clap of thunder punctuated the close. Daniel sighed as his mum's head poked into the hallway. She looked at him for a few seconds, didn't say anything, then disappeared back into the lounge.

Daniel hesitated before following her. He found his mum sitting in the chair by the lampshade, the same one he'd been waiting in during her date the other night.

'You were meant to be home by four o'clock.'

'What time is it?' asked Daniel.

'Four-thirty.'

Daniel scratched the back of his head. 'I'm sorry.'

'Sorry's not good enough.'

'I apologise.'

'It's not your terminology, Daniel, it's the fact your sister is...' She choked on her words, taking a few moments to compose herself. 'This is not the time to be gallivanting around the village with your friends.'

'We weren't gallivanting,' said Daniel, although he had no idea what the word 'gallivanting' meant. 'We were looking.'

'You don't go looking on your own, you stay with the group.'

Since Daria had gone missing, his mum's face had been growing paler by the hour. At this point, it didn't look like there was any blood left in her at all. Like you could cut her, and all she'd bleed would be tears.

'I want you to stay close,' she said softly, twiddling the ring on her finger. 'I want you to stay with me.'

Daniel nodded and said, 'Okay', although they both knew it wasn't going to happen. His sister was gone, yes, but a boy couldn't change his nature any more than a leopard could change its spots. It may have been wrong, but even if the sky was falling down and the world was ending, a boy's last moments would be with his friends, not with his family. And that was just the truth of it. Apart from that, Daniel could see there was a part of her that knew he'd be alright. Even though she was one child down and a breath away from weeping inconsolably. She knew. Lightning didn't strike the same spot twice. And whatever had happened to Daria had happened to her. Specifically.

In her eyes, Daniel could see her straining to find the reason why, and for a moment, he thought about telling her what he knew. But then he remembered what Terry had said, about her own parents being taken by The Ogle. She'd never seen them again, and while she seemed strong, and secure, and alive, Daniel wasn't sure he could survive the same fate. Lightning didn't strike the same spot, sure, but The Ogle wasn't like any normal storm. The Ogle was a storm that played by its own rules.

Instead, Daniel stood, turned on the television, and curled up beside his mum. They sat in silence until she fell asleep, listening more to the rain than they were the telly.

Once his mother was snoring, Daniel carefully lifted her head from his shoulder and turned off the television. He wandered into the kitchen and lifted a sausage roll from the fridge. He thought he was hungry, but when he saw the row of baked beans reserved for Daria on the second shelf, his appetite vanished, and he only managed a few bites. Throwing the rest in the bin, he poured himself a glass of water and headed upstairs. When he passed Daria's room, he took a moment to look inside. The room was tidy, just as Daria had left it, and her bed was made. It would have been hard to tell the room belonged to a child at all, if it weren't for the tufts of cotton scattered across the carpet and sheets. Her teddy bear was propped against the pillow, staring at Daniel and waiting for another story. One that wouldn't come.

Again, Daniel found himself fighting back tears. He closed the door gently and walked into his own bedroom. Once there, he sat down on his bed and stared at the wall for a few seconds. He had a poster there of his favourite band, Gorillaz, and below that, a desk topped with CDs, his Walkman, and a load of books he'd never read. He thought about picking one up now to try take his mind off things. But while he liked to tell the stories, reading them had never been of much interest to him. He always found his mind wandering elsewhere, to a tale of his own making, and the same was true for his day-to-day life. In fact, his day-to-day life was mostly spent trying to find his own story. That was the reason he'd gone back to The Ogle House. There was no better story than one being lived, and that was the same for every kid. Only now he was sitting here, alone on his bed, without Daria in the next room, and he wished more than anything he'd never turned that first page.

Still holding back tears, he turned around and climbed under the covers. He thought it would be impossible to fall asleep. For the last two nights, he'd only managed a few hours, and so he planned to simply lie down and think about the blue spiral. But with the rain pattering against the window, and the soft rumble of thunder vibrating the sky every few seconds, his lack of rest quickly caught up with him. Daniel closed his eyes, and when he did, sleep wrapped over him like a second blanket, sending him into a deep abyss. With no nightmares. No dreams.

Only it didn't last long. After just a few hours, Daniel awoke to something hard hitting his bedroom window. At first, he thought the storm outside had started to hail, but the tapping was infrequent. It sounded like someone was targeting his window with tiny stones. He climbed out of his bed and saw Jamie Watt staring up at him on his driveway.

'What the hell...' Daniel slid open his window and ducked as another stone hurtled past him. 'Damn it, Jamie! I can see you! You don't have to keep throwing pebbles at me!'

'Sorry! Listen, I need to talk to you!'

Daniel glanced at the clock on his bedside table. It was nearing midnight, yet Jamie looked like he was about to ask Daniel on a country hike. He was wearing an oversized Barbour jacket, likely belonging to his father, and on his feet were a pair of wellington boots.

'I've had an idea about the spiral,' he said, straining to be heard over another rumble of thunder. 'We need to speak with Terry. It's urgent.'

'Can't it wait until morning?' replied Daniel.

'Can Daria?'

If it was anyone else standing below him, Daniel would have had a strong mind to slam the window shut and climb back into bed. But Jamie wasn't the impulsive sort. He was a well-mannered boy who, visits to The Ogle House aside, didn't like to bend the rules. To be standing here after dark, alone, there must have been a good reason. And Daniel wanted to hear it. After just a moment of hesitation, he grabbed his raincoat from the cupboard and headed downstairs, careful not to wake his mum as he put on his shoes.

When he exited onto the driveway, Jamie grabbed him by the sleeve and whisked him down the road. It was only when they reached the outskirts of Argos Farm and Jamie went to retrieve a torch from his pocket that Daniel actually got a moment to speak.

'Jamie!' He panted. 'What the hell is going on? This isn't like you.'

'Shh!'

Jamie raised a finger to his lips, then pointed slowly at the road ahead. It was empty, save for a small bus stop beside the gate to the field. Sitting inside that bus stop were two dark figures, a thin trail of smoke eking from beneath their hoods.

'The Mumford Boys...' Daniel whispered.

'Come on.' Jamie grabbed his wrist again, climbing over the stiles onto the farm.

'Do you think they saw us?' Daniel asked.

'I don't know.'

'Okay, so tell me what we're doing.'

'Did you not notice the garden of St Martha's House backs onto Argos Farm? I figured it'd be easier to get in that way. More subtle.'

'I mean, why are we going there in the first place?'

'Oh, well, I had some thoughts earlier this evening. I was going over everything Terry had said, and something occurred to me. Potentially something big. But it'll sound stupid if we don't talk to Terry first. I need to know I didn't misremember. I mean, I have a pretty good memory. Maybe it's from reading all those books. But with everything that's been going on, I don't know, I'm starting to doubt myself.'

Upon reaching the other side of Argos Farm, Daniel took a quick glance back to check they weren't followed, then he and Jamie clambered over the fence into the back garden of St Martha's House.

'How are we supposed to get to her?' Daniel asked uncertainly.

'Don't worry.' Jamie gave his pocket a shake. 'I picked up some pebbles from your driveway.'

Jamie led him towards the back of the house, but before he could pull the stones from his shorts, something stopped him. A familiar voice, coming from one of the flower beds.

'I'll stay out this time — Wanker! Fuck off! Fuck off, fuck off! — I'll get wet, I don't care.'

Jamie aimed his torch to the left and illuminated Terry Bantam.

'Who's there?' she called out.

'It's just us,' said Daniel.

Terry remained dead still, watching them as they approached. Daniel noticed she was shaking. Judging by how drenched her clothes were, she must've been standing out in the storm for ages. She didn't even have shoes on.

'What are you doing here?' she asked.

'We came to talk to you,' Daniel replied. 'What are *you* doing here? You're soaked.'

'I thought I — Fuck off, fuck off! Shit! — I thought I told you to meet me tomorrow.'

'You did,' said Jamie. 'It's just... I wanted to ask you something.'

'Jesus. It must be important.'

'It is. I mean, I think it is. But...' Jamie was staring at her blue hair, which was sitting like two damp rags upon her shoulders. 'Do you want to go inside first?'

'Spit it out, nerdy birdy.'

Jamie jumped a little. 'Uhh, okay. The spiral. Maybe I'm overthinking it, but I was going over what you said. Every part of what you said. I thought about it all evening. I even wrote it out, and I —'

'I meant spit out the point.'

Jamie spluttered. He was still nervous, and that made Daniel slightly nervous too.

'Right,' he said shakily. 'Yes, the point. You don't remember a lot about what happened. But you said it was blue. The spiral,

I mean. And cold. And when you saw your parents, how did you describe them?'

'I said I saw them staring at me.'

'And reaching down, is that right?'

Terry shrugged. 'Yeah. So?'

'What are you getting at?' asked Daniel.

'I'm doing what Terry told me to do,' said Jamie defensively. 'I'm looking beneath the surface. Her parents reached *down*. I was thinking that was a strange thing to say. But it made me realise something. We were thinking the portal must be something in front of us, right? Like something you can walk into. But if that were true, you wouldn't have described it like that. You would have said they reached *out*.'

A flash of lightning lit the clouds above them, followed by a distant rumble of thunder about seven seconds after. The storm was slowly easing off.

'I still don't understand,' said Daniel.

'I think we've seen the spiral,' Jamie replied impatiently. 'I think we all have.'

'Like you said before, I think I would have noticed something like that.'

'Except you wouldn't, because it's a part of Deanshire. See, if something like this really existed, it would create a ripple effect. It would alter gravity, for a start. Electromagnetic fields, spatial distortions. All that. I read all about it last year, in a book about wormholes by Kit Thorne. He explained everything that might happen, and what's the one place in Deanshire that people can't explain?'

Terry tilted her head, like she might have misheard him. But Daniel had heard him just fine. And he knew exactly what Jamie meant.

'The fishing hole,' he muttered.

Jamie nodded. 'I think there's a reason the fishing hole exists. I think there's a reason we see fish swimming in a circle.' He held out his hand, ticking off each point with his fingers. 'A blue spiral. Cold. Her parents reached down to get her. It all fits.'

'The fishing hole,' said Terry slowly. 'I've heard about that. Where is it?'

'It's a spot in the River Rocker,' Jamie replied. 'Near the old railway bridge. And I think it could be —'

'The old railway bridge. That's about thirty minutes away on foot, right?'

'Uhh, yeah.'

Giving her hair a quick shake, Terry turned and walked towards the house, her bare feet making sludgy noises in the grass.

Jamie gawped at her. 'Wait. Are we going now?'

'Well, not *right* now. I'm not going without my shoes. Hold on...' She stopped just before she reached the doors. 'Do either of you fish?'

Daniel hesitated. 'Curtis does. Sometimes. Manchester tries to.'

'Good. We're gonna need his rod. And we may as well bring Manchester. That'll make two.'

'But we can't go now,' Jamie argued. 'It's dark and it's pouring down.'

'We're getting wet either way, nerdy birdy.'

'But... But...'

Jamie stuttered, glancing back at Daniel with a glint of hope in his eyes, as if he was waiting for him to argue too. But Daniel remained silent.

'You can wipe that scared look off your face,' said Terry. 'Because I'm telling you, Daniel's sister will be scared-er. That's why we're gonna go get her. Right now. This second. So... Fuck! Shit! Wanker!'

Terry broke down into another barrage of tics. It lasted for what felt like forever. Then, almost as suddenly as they had started, the tics stopped and her face went back to normal again. She took a few breaths and composed herself.

'... so let's get a shift on,' she finished.

And then she raced inside St Martha's House, leaving the pair of them alone and shivering in the darkness of the garden.

That was when the rain stopped.

THE AFTERNOON, 18 JUNE 2073

When Daniel got back from the bathroom, the stranger was standing by the door onto the garden, his forehead pressed against the glass. He stayed that way while Daniel made more coffee, and even when he sat down beside him, the man didn't move. If it had been anyone else, or under any other circumstances, Daniel might've asked what the hell he was playing at. But as it was, he was just thankful for the respite.

He'd been talking for several hours now, and he'd probably said more in that time than he had all year. Barring his trips to the store, and his brief words of reprimand to his cat, Daniel didn't feel the need to speak. He'd heard other people talked to themselves, and that was just fine. But Daniel had said everything he'd wanted to say in his life. Anything he said now was just afters. A petit four. Even the story he was telling was just regurgitated words, all of which had been said and felt many years ago. Nothing was original anymore.

'Sorry,' the stranger finally spoke up. 'I was miles away.'

Daniel wiped his eyes. 'No, it's my fault. I'm surprised I haven't been going to the bathroom more often. It's a curse of my BPH.'

The stranger looked at him awkwardly. He didn't linger on the subject. He sat down opposite and pressed his elbows on the table.

'So, you went to pick up Manchester and Curtis?'

Daniel nodded. 'And Buster. Manchester was intent on taking him with us.'

'Because of the Mumford Boys?'

'I think because it was dark.'

The door of the kitchen creaked a little as Junebug pushed her way back in. She'd spent the last twenty minutes following a blue fly, waiting for it to buzz low enough to catch, but she must have given up because the fly followed in after her. She watched it boredly for a second, then returned to Daniel's lap.

'I'm interested that you mentioned them,' said the stranger.

'Why? It doesn't mean anything. You asked for all the details, and I'm determined to give them to you.'

He said it as sincerely as he could, but they both knew the Mumford Boys had a bigger part to play yet. The stranger knew it because he was smart, and cunning, and he could see the plot twists before they arrived. Daniel knew it because he had lived it, and felt it, and he remembered. The curse of retelling this particular story was that there was a story to tell in the first place.

He leant back and began stroking Junebug's head. He felt her little heart beating fast against his leg, so he tapped her chest, slower and slower, until the rhythm of her heart matched him. That was when she drifted off to sleep.

Chapter Ten

UNDER THE BED

Daniel, Manchester, Jamie, Curtis, Terry, and Buster walked east along the railway track to Tidebrook and the old railway bridge. Forty years ago, they would have been walking on a live track called the Cuckoo Line, which travelled all the way from Station Road to Sandhog. But after the Beeching Axe of 1963, it was shut down and only used again to transport kegs between The White Rose and Tackle Brewery in the 1980s. That only lasted until the Beer Orders of 1989, though, which resulted in the closing of The White Rose, and a few years later, Tackle too. Then it was just a line of rusty bullheads again, and while that was a bad example of Britain's ability to look after its own, it did provide Daniel and his friends with an easy route to the fishing hole — without the fear of being run over in the process.

They had been walking for twenty minutes. Curtis had a fishing rod in his hand, Daniel had a backpack slung over one shoulder, and Jamie led the rest of them with his torch. They would have been there already if it hadn't been for Manchester's protestations. In the beginning, he'd been a surefire no-go, but the thought of breaking the rules turned out to be too tempting to resist. He followed them from the back, keeping quiet and avoiding contact with Terry, who didn't quite do the same thing. The closer they got to the fishing hole, the worse her Tourette's got. Sheep boy, king of the klutzes (that was a new one for Curtis), nerdy birdy, boogerman. The four boys were being called every name under the sun, and it was only when she got so loud that Buster would start barking ('STUPID MANGY MUTT, YOU'RE A MOP WITH LEGS!') that she would stop and start whistling.

Her third bout had just ended and, fearing another tirade would start any minute, Manchester ran to the front to walk alongside Jamie.

'Can I help you?' Jamie said after a few seconds.

'Yes, actually. Where did you read this thing about the fishing hole again?'

'I didn't read about the fishing hole. I put two and two together. It was a book about wormholes by Kit Thorne. I read it last year while waiting for my comic.'

'You remembered something you read in a science book a whole year ago? Jesus, you're wasted on comics.'

Jamie didn't reply. He kept his eyes on the tracks. The sound of rushing water was growing louder, so they must have been close. Daniel looked back at Terry nervously. It was fine now, but if they really were getting close to The Ogle's lair, he couldn't help but feel their approach might be a little obvious. Being stealthy with Tourette's was like playing hide and seek with the BFG, and a good part of him thought it might be wise for Terry to stay behind. But then, he would never say that to her. In fact, he would rather die and be gobbled up by The Ogle than say that to her.

Terry's face contorted. 'FUCKING SHEEP BOY, LOOKING AT ME LIKE A FAGGOT!'

The last word was almost sung, and she squeezed her eyes shut. Buster peered up at her disapprovingly.

'Sorry,' she said after a few pops and whistles.

'You don't have to apologise,' said Daniel.

'I don't actually use that word. You know, in normal conversation — FUCKING FAGGOTY FAG-FACE! GONNA PICK THEM STRAWBERRIES LIKE A —'

Buster started barking and Terry managed to cut herself off, making some more popping sounds before rubbing and tapping her chest. She took a deep breath, one more pop for luck, and then fell silent.

'Can I ask you something about it?' Daniel asked. 'Your Tourette's, I mean.'

'Don't you have other stuff on your mind?'

'Sure, it's just...' Daniel bit his lip, wondering if there was any delicate way of asking this. 'Why do you keep mentioning strawberries?'

'How d'you mean — STRAWBERRIES IN A HAT, GONNA FUCKING MASH 'EM!'

'That. You say it quite a lot. I mean, I understand all the swearing. At least, I guess I do. But how do strawberries fit into it?'

'It's an impulse thing,' said Terry hoarsely. 'There's no meaning to it. It just feels right. That's what they tell me anyway. My brain gets an auditory satisfaction from saying it —

FUCKING STRAWBERRIES IN A HAT! SHEEP BOY AND THE MOPPY DOG! FUCK OFF, FUCK OFF! FUCK. OFF!' She coughed, rubbing her chest for a whole minute this time. 'I'm glad it's satisfied,' she eventually finished.

'Can I ask you something else?' Daniel said.

'Go ahead,' replied Terry.

'What were you doing when we found you? Why were you standing outside in the rain?'

Before Terry could say anything, Jamie yelled out, 'We're here!', and Daniel turned to see the old railway bridge in front of them.

It wasn't a large bridge. The river itself was just twenty feet across, and the bridge curled over it in an arch, just about wide enough to let a single carriage pass. They stopped and stared at it for a few seconds. Manchester gave Jamie a hearty thump on the arm.

'Wanna be louder?' he hissed. 'I don't think The Ogle heard you.'

'Sorry,' Jamie whispered back.

They proceeded forwards. As they got closer, Daniel made out the weeds and nettles that had crawled through the gaps in the timber, and he rued the fact he was about to add more stings to his growing collection. He didn't make a fuss out of it, though. None of them did. Making no sound except the occasional clangs of shoes against steel, they crept carefully onto the bridge and peered into the water.

'There it is!' Jamie said almost as soon as the torchlight hit the surface. 'I see it!'

The five of them huddled together and followed Jamie's finger. The light of the torch was shining right in the middle of the river, where scores of large, dark fish were swirling around in a circle.

'How are we supposed to reach from up here?' Manchester turned to Terry. 'Your parents must have had incredibly long arms.'

'Tell you what,' Terry replied. 'Why don't you get a few stretches in? That can be Plan B if Plan A doesn't work out. Give me the fishing rod, Curtis...' She held out her hand and Curtis passed it over obligingly. 'Now, Daniel, give me the bait.'

Daniel shrugged off his backpack and rummaged inside. When Terry had told him her plan, he'd known almost immediately what the perfect bait would be. Thankfully, his mother had still been asleep when he went to retrieve it. Manchester gawped as he pulled Daria's teddy bear out of the bag and handed it over.

'A teddy bear?'

'It's her favourite.'

'This is insane. We're literally fishing for Daniel's sister.'

'So start stretching,' said Terry.

With her tongue sticking out in concentration, she wrapped the fishing line around the bear's neck, giving it a few good tugs to make sure it was firm. As she did so, a tuft of stuffing fell from the gap in its belly. Daniel grabbed it. He'd pulled the rest of the stuffing out and replaced it with stones from his driveway, so that must have been the last of it. He wasn't sure why, but he gave it a quick kiss and stuffed it in his back pocket. Then he watched as

Terry positioned the rod on the parapet and began unreeling the bear towards the river.

'Come on,' she whispered. 'All you need to do is grab hold of it. Just like I did.'

The seconds went by, and the teddy bear dropped lower, its body limp and sad looking. In a weird sort of way, it looked like it was being hanged for a crime. It would have deserved it, Daniel thought. Teddy bears were meant to protect their owners from the nightmares, and clearly this one hadn't done a great job of that. As the teddy bear plopped into the water, Daniel reckoned this was its chance to set things right.

The five of them waited nervously, their ears prickling as Terry continued to feed out the line. Ten more seconds went by. Then twenty. Then thirty. Pretty soon, a whole minute had passed, and Terry was still unreeling.

'How deep is this river?' she asked uncertainly.

'Not sure,' whispered Curtis.

Another minute passed. Daniel kept his eyes on the fishing hole. Perhaps it was the torchlight, or perhaps it was just his eyes playing tricks on him, but he could have sworn this part of the river was different from the rest of it. The torchlight was making it glow, sure, but the colour of that glow was strange. Like a pale, cloudy turquoise, made even more eerie by the faint wisp of fog that was hovering above the surface.

'Could be the current is taking it?' said Jamie.

'Unlikely,' Daniel said. 'That thing's weighed way down.'

Terry stopped unreeling, placing the butt of the rod onto the ground, wedged between the dirt and one of the sleepers of the railway track.

'I'm gonna stop there. Don't wanna run out of — Fucking! Shit! Prick! — don't wanna run out of line.'

Daniel stared at the tip, hoping beyond hope that it would start twitching. Only it didn't. The rod was completely motionless, the line tense and still like a needle. Buster started sniffing at Daniel's feet, then he did the same to Terry, then Manchester. He trotted between them as if he was worried they'd all turned to stone. In many ways, they had. The five of them were as still as the line, waiting with bated breath for any sign that there was something at the end of it.

Around them, the world kept moving. Chirps and owl hoots filtered out of the woodland, and every now and then, the branches bristled, sending waves of damp smelling leaves on the breeze. Beyond the woodland and the river, there was the faint sound of a road (probably Dunwick Road, if Daniel had to guess), with cars rushing along it every thirty or so seconds. The longer they stood there, the more alive the world around them became, until Daniel was sure he could hear the woodlice moving beneath his feet.

That was until Manchester broke the spell.

'Well, this was a big bust,' he said with a distinct air of the *I told you so*'s resting in his voice.

'You don't know that yet,' said Daniel.

'I know we just dunked a teddy bear in the water and absolutely nothing happened. Why did I get dragged out of bed for this?'

'Have you got something against me, boogerman?' said Terry.

'Stop calling me that.'

'Stop getting boogers.'

'I only got one, and —'

'Guys,' Jamie interrupted, 'we shouldn't fight. Not if The Ogle can hear us.'

Manchester scoffed. 'It isn't down there, Jamie. And even if it is, all we've done is give it a stocking filler. Some rescue mission this is.'

Terry glared at him. 'I'm starting to get tired of your tone, boogerman.'

'I'm starting to get tired of you. I mean, what are you even doing here? I think I know.'

'Enlighten me, O' Great Mystical One.'

'You don't have any friends, so you've decided to latch onto our party. And you're using his missing sister to do it.'

Manchester pointed at Daniel, but Terry kept her gaze firmly on him, her hands tensing around the fishing rod.

'Oh yeah,' she said mockingly. 'I really want to be your friend. You're literally eleven years old, you wank-stain.'

'Oh, go talk to a slug.'

Manchester turned and began pacing back towards the woodland. Both Curtis and Terry called after him.

'Manchester! Where —'

'WANKER!'

'— are —'

'PRICK!'

'— you —'

'FUCK OFF!'

'— going?'

'Don't lose your head,' shouted Manchester. 'I'm just going for a whizz.'

He shouldered through a pile of shrubs and disappeared from view. Terry blew a raspberry (or perhaps it was another tic, Daniel wasn't sure) and then turned back to the river. She didn't say anything, but even in the darkness, Daniel could tell she was upset.

'I don't think that's why you're doing this,' he said as encouragingly as possible. 'Also, if you did want to be our friend, I'd be cool with it.'

'Yeah, and me,' said Curtis.

Terry tried to appear nonplussed, but there was a flicker of a smile on her lips that betrayed her. It stayed there for a few seconds before being tugged away, just at the same moment the fishing line was tugged too.

'Holy shit,' Jamie whispered. 'Is that...'

The rod bent violently. It sank fast towards the ground, and the butt was jerked out of position, the line beginning to unreel.

'There's something there,' said Terry. 'Grab the line, Curtis.'

Curtis clicked into action, jumping over the rails to take hold of the fishing line a few inches from the tip. Jamie did the same thing, stuffing his torch into his jacket pocket and grabbing the line lower down, where it stretched taut over the edge. The tip of the rod held, the load taken off, and Terry positioned herself behind it.

'Okay,' she said confidently. 'Now one, two, three, pull!'

Curtis and Jamie heaved the line towards them, and Terry retreated, bringing the rod with her. Daniel snatched the torch from Jamie's pocket and pointed it towards the fishing hole.

Buster joined him, placing both paws on the parapet excitedly, his tail wagging. A couple of bubbles popped on the surface. Terry called out again.

'One, two, three, pull!'

They each repeated the motion, pulling the line up another few inches.

'Could be a fish,' Jamie panted.

'That's one big fish,' said Curtis.

'It's her,' Terry said assuredly. 'Keep pulling.'

'GUYS!'

Manchester came running out of the undergrowth, his arms waving frantically.

'Still think I wanna be your friend, booger —' Terry began but was cut off by Buster's barking. 'Oi, I didn't swear at him!'

'No!' Manchester cried. 'I saw them in the woods. It's...'

Daniel swung the torch to the woodland just as the Mumford Boys walked out of the trees and onto the railway line. *No*, he thought desperately. *Not them. Not now.*

'What are you running for, Manchester?' asked Marcus. 'Did we catch you with your pants down?'

As he got closer, Daniel noticed the bandage over his left eye. Likewise, his brother Matt was walking with a slight limp, a strip of white bandage poking out from underneath his left trouser leg.

'Oh shit.' Jamie took a step backwards. 'They must have followed us.'

Daniel pointed at the line. 'Don't let go!' he cried frantically.

'Doing a spot of fishing are we?' Matt stopped with his hands behind his back. 'Oh, and with a girlfriend too. Very romantic.'

'FUCK OFF!'

The words came out of Terry's mouth loudly, and Daniel felt his heart sink.

'What was that?' asked Marcus.

'FUCK OFF! FUCKING DEADBEAT DADS IN WAITING! FUCK OFF!'

'Why don't you say that to my face?' Marcus reached down and retrieved a familiar-looking knife from his pocket. The blade flashed and glinted in the torchlight.

'No!' Daniel shouted. 'She didn't mean it! She has a thing! Terry, please!'

But Terry's eyes were clamped shut, her hands trembling and her head twitching from side to side.

'FUCKING WANKERS! WANKERS, WANKERS, WANKERS!'

From the look of her face, there was a strong chance she knew who these people were and what they could do, but she couldn't stop herself. She cursed at them over and over, and didn't stop even when Marcus pointed the knife directly at her.

'We came here for them, but we'll be happy to cut you up too.'

In the corner of Daniel's vision, he could see the line slipping out of Curtis and Jamie's grip. He looked back towards the river helplessly and found himself grabbing Jamie's elbow, forcing him to stay in place. Terry continued to swear and spit, and Marcus Mumford rushed forward, his knife raised. Before he could get near her, though, Manchester shouted and kicked Buster hard on the hind leg.

'BUSTER! SIC 'EM!'

And Buster leapt into action.

With his lips curled and his teeth shining, he charged towards Marcus, and Daniel felt a pang of relief. Only the relief was short-lived. Just as Buster got within a few feet of his target, Matt pulled his hands from behind his back and threw what looked like a large, dark cloud into the air.

All of a sudden, Buster was writhing between the rails, turning and wrenching as if he'd been put under some kind of spell. Manchester yelled and Daniel pulled the torch down to the ground. The dark cloud was actually a large, thick fishing net, which was coiled around Buster and causing him to yap, bite, and twist.

Matt whooped in triumph. 'GOT HIM! YOU STUPID PRICKS, YOU DIDN'T THINK WE'D BE READY THIS TIME?! DUNK HIM, MARCUS!'

Obeying the order, Marcus lifted Buster into the air, his arm curled around his neck. Buster struggled against him and tried his hardest to bite, but Marcus was too quick. In what felt like a second, he was already at the side of the bridge, slamming Buster down onto the parapet before pushing him over the edge. The tangled mass of netting fell towards the river and disappeared from view with an almighty splash.

'BUSTER!' Manchester shouted.

Jamie pulled himself from Daniel's grasp. 'WE'VE GOTTA LEG IT, DANIEL!'

He let go of the line and sprinted in the opposite direction, and Curtis did the same. At the same moment, the rod bent, and the line snapped. Daniel screamed in desperation and tried to grab it, but he was too slow. The surface of the fishing hole bubbled and frothed, and the line disappeared into the centre of it. Terry started running too, her hands around her head and the curses continuing to pour out of her mouth. Daniel expected Manchester to be next, but when he turned, he saw that he was grappling with Marcus, one hand around his wrist while the other landed a hard blow to his face. He ducked as Matt slashed at him, then Marcus kicked him in the groin, and he tumbled backwards.

'MANCHESTER!' Daniel shouted.

Marcus pulled his knife down, and Daniel could have sworn he was aiming for Manchester's face. Before he could reach his target, however, Manchester twisted to the side of the bridge and vaulted over the parapet, aiming for the exact same spot Buster had just landed.

And Daniel did the same. Without taking a moment to think about it, he leapt onto the wall of the bridge and jumped towards the fishing hole, squeezing his eyes shut as his body breached the surface and the spiral swallowed him up.

The water felt different to what he expected. Being the dead of night, it should have been cold and stinging, and his body should have been frozen in a state of shock. That's what had happened two years ago, when he and his friends had gone diving at Pelos Pool, just outside Deanshire. He remembered being eaten by that water. Chewed up and spat out, with his bones quivering and his heart thumping. But the water he'd just dived into wasn't only warm, it didn't really feel like water at all.

For a long time, it felt like Daniel was falling. Falling and falling and falling through nothing but thick-feeling air. He had felt the surface. He had felt his body crashing through it But after that, the world around him had turned into a void. Completely silent.

When Daniel opened his eyes, all he saw was dark. No weeds, no fish, no life. Even when he held his hand in front of him and tried to make out the shape of his fingers, there was just a blank, empty space. He was holding his breath, but a part of him reckoned he didn't need to. Like he could open his lungs and breathe in this new and strange world, and there would be no water to fill them. Even in his heightened state of anxiety and confusion, however, he was aware that, while there was a chance no water would fill them, there was also a chance no air would fill them either. So he kept his breath tight in his chest, the bottle cap screwed firmly shut. And he kept falling.

He assumed he was falling because his arms were up above his head, and he could feel the weight of his body dragging him down. But he didn't know for sure, so he kept his eyes open, looking for something, *anything*, to indicate where he was or where he was going.

Eventually he spotted it. Below him, on what might have been the riverbed. A light. It started out small, just a speck of whiteness in the black of the void. But it grew into something larger. A thick white dot was ballooning below Daniel's feet, like a giant mouth opening wide and sucking him down into a gullet.

And then there was something else. Another figure, dark and distant, spinning in a spiral and being sucked down along with him. For a moment, Daniel thought it might be Daria, and he had a sudden urge to turn himself upside down and try to grab her. Only his arms remained above his head, and for some reason, he couldn't control them. All he could do was watch as the figure sank deeper and deeper, and the white light, which had now engulfed the entirety of the riverbed, shone a light onto its features.

It wasn't Daria. It was Buster. Out of the fishing net now and fighting to swim back to the surface. The more he struggled, however, the deeper he seemed to fall, until he was right on the precipice of the light, and something else arrived to meet him.

Out of the light. A pair of hands. Huge, dreadful, stark white hands, with long, spindly fingers, and sharp, cracked nails. They closed around Buster and cupped him into their palms, like they were catching a butterfly.

Daniel opened his mouth and let out a loud but silent scream. As he did so, the hands retreated, Buster still inside them, and the white light disappeared. Then the sharp, all-encompassing blackness Daniel had come to know wrapped around him once more. And finally, almost to his relief, it sent him cold.

THE EVENING, 18 JUNE 2073

The kitchen was bright, but for a moment during Daniel's story, it went as dark as the River Rocker. The stranger's face disappeared, the mug in his hand, the table. Everything faded into a state of black, causing a ball of anxiety to coil in Daniel's gut. He tried to get over it by closing his eyes and rubbing his chest, just as Terry would do when she fell into one of her tics. But it didn't work. He'd been so engrossed in his own tale that he'd started reliving it, and now he was stuck in the darkness. Just as he'd been back in that fishing hole.

And the whole thing made him laugh. Just a little. Before starting this story, Daniel had assumed there was enough distance between him and his childhood that it wouldn't affect him. That he could tell it but not feel it. Only he couldn't have been more wrong. Whether it was the thrash of the sun, the smell of the pollen, the sting of the water, the bite of blood. 2004, 2005, 2006. Happiness, sadness, blackness. It had all been sleeping in his veins, waiting to be woken up. And Daniel had indeed woken it.

He laughed some more, and as he did so, the anxiety eked away. He shook his head and cursed himself for being so naive. To think that memories could die and the warmth of that summer could fade. It was moronic. As Jamie had once told him, the light of the sun travelled ninety-three million miles to reach earth, and so it was only natural that its warmth could linger, could seep into the skin and reawaken the soul of a senile old fool who thought he'd never feel it again. He scratched his hands and thought to himself: *How long is the road to Castletown?*

But he must have said it aloud, because when he opened his eyes and saw the stranger again, he smiled and said back,

'How long?'

Chapter Eleven

SURPRISED!

The first time Daniel Ottoman awoke, he was still in the fishing hole. The world around him was pitch black, but somehow, he knew it was spinning. He could feel the blood in his head sloshing from one side to the other, his body twisting in a hurricane, circling round and round like he was just another fish to catch.

The second time felt different. Things were still dark, but the spinning had stopped, and he could sense tiny, short breaths escaping from his lungs. The third time he woke up, he could see things. There was a white light in the centre of his vision, and for a second, he thought it might be the light from the fishing hole again. Like a pair of huge hands would appear through it and snatch him up at any moment. But then he heard the low, mechanical buzz of a dying bulb, and the world around him became more real.

He was out of the fishing hole, he realised that. He was out and in a world he didn't quite know yet. Perhaps his own. Perhaps The Ogle's. For all Daniel knew, he had sunk into the portal and crossed to the other side, and that meant his sister was close. With all the strength he could muster, he tried to reach out and see if he could touch her. But all he could feel were soft pillows and sheets that, for some reason, he knew were white. He looked down and confirmed it. Daniel was lying on a narrow bed, wrapped in blankets, and attached by some sticky pads to a device that went beep every few seconds. To his right was a window, the blinds half-shut, and to his left there was a door. From where he was lying, it looked like there was a painting a few inches above the handle. A self-portrait of his mother, staring at him with soft, sparkling eyes, and her skin pulled taut, like the artist had used a brush that was just a little too thin.

The illusion was spoiled when the door opened and his mother stepped inside. When she did so, those sparkling eyes overfilled and she began weeping. She walked towards Daniel's bed and bundled him up into a breathless hug. Her fingers seeped through his hair, and again, Daniel could smell the flowery perfume of her own. She grabbed a remote control from the railing of the bed and pressed one of the buttons. A few seconds later, a nurse entered the room and began asking him questions.

'Can you tell me your name? / Do you remember what happened? / Are you in any pain? / Do you feel cold?'

The questions came one after the other, but it felt like they all came at the same time. Daniel couldn't answer any of them. Looking concerned, the nurse left the room and came back with a male doctor, who asked the same questions again, only while fiddling with the wires on Daniel's chest. He said something about giving him time, then dimmed the lights, asked the nurse to sit in for a while, and left. The nurse sat down and talked about her garden, and as she did so, everything steadily got clearer. When the nurse recognised the change, she asked him the questions again, and this time, Daniel answered all of them but one.

He remained silent about what happened. Not because he was afraid to tell her, but because he didn't quite know himself. He remembered diving into the fishing hole. He remembered seeing the bright light, and Buster, and those dreadful white hands wrapping around him. But he couldn't make any sense of it. They were just images. Horrifying pictures that spiralled around his head as quickly as he'd spiralled down the fishing hole, and even when his mum and the nurse left the room, and he had time to piece them together, nothing got any clearer. After a few minutes, his mother came back and asked the question again, but Daniel remained silent. She pulled up a chair and stroked his hand.

'It's okay, Daniel. You can talk about it. We know what happened out of the water anyway.'

Daniel suddenly remembered the predicament he'd left his friends in. 'Jamie! Curtis! Are they alright?'

'They're fine. Manchester too. You owe him your life, he's the one who pulled you out of the water.'

Daniel blinked. While he should have been gracious that Manchester had saved his life, any emotion was quickly overruled by a sudden new question. The last time he'd seen Manchester, he had just dived into the River Rocker to save Buster. If he'd been the one to save him, perhaps he'd seen what Daniel had seen. If that was the case, there was no chance Manchester could deny that Terry had been right. What's more, there was no chance anyone could say Daniel had been hallucinating, which, if it was just him on his own, he was sure they'd do. He bit his lip, contemplating the possibility. He had to ask Manchester as soon as he saw him, but for now, there was an even more pressing question.

'What about Terry?' he asked. When his mother stared at him blankly, he clarified, 'Esther, I mean.'

'Who's Esther?'

'She's...'

Daniel started, but he didn't finish. If his mother didn't know who Terry was, that meant there was a good chance she had got away. Not wanting to get her into trouble, Daniel didn't linger on it.

'Daniel,' his mother resumed her questioning. 'We need to know everything that happened. Jamie said you were attacked by those Mumford kids. Did they push you into the river?'

Daniel hesitated, wondering exactly how much of the story Jamie had told.

'It's okay,' said his mum. 'You don't have to worry about them anymore. Your friends are smart. They called the police as soon as they could. Both Marcus and Matt are in a detention centre right now, and if they get out, Mrs Mumford will take them straight to their dad in London. You won't have to see them again. If that's what you're worried about —'

'Have they found Buster?' Daniel asked suddenly, though he already knew the answer.

'Not yet.'

'They won't find him.'

His mother looked at him curiously, faint lines of concern creasing her worn and tired face. She squeezed his hand.

'Daniel, you need to tell us if it was the Mumford kids who pushed you in. If we want them to be punished for this, then that will be a big part of it. They had knives, they tried to kill an innocent animal, if they tried to kill you too —'

'I'm not worried about the Mumford Boys,' said Daniel. 'I'm worried about Daria.'

His mother faltered. 'Jamie said that you went looking for her. Why did you think she was there?'

Daniel looked at her guardedly. 'It's complicated...'

For a while, the beeps of the heart rate monitor took over the conversation. His mum stood up, crossed her arms, and dug her chin into her chest.

'Listen, I want you to know I don't blame you for what you did. Everything that's been happening, it's taken a strain on you. Of course it has. Right now, I'm just happy you're alive. The thought that I could have lost another...' She trailed off, her hands beginning to shake a little bit. Under the bright light of the ceiling bulb, she looked almost like a ghost. Only without any of the glow or sparkle. 'But you can't do things like this on your own. If you thought there was a chance she could be there, if you had any kind of inkling, you should have sat down and talked to me.'

'You wouldn't have listened,' said Daniel.

'Of course I would have listened.'

'Then you wouldn't have cared.'

His mother's gaze lifted abruptly. As if he was on auto-mode, Daniel went to apologise. But something made him reconsider. It was hard to tell, seeing as he was lying in a hospital bed, still dizzy from the night before and feeling sick, but Daniel was beginning to realise he was angry. Right there, along with the sickness and disorientation, there was a rumbling fury spreading through his bones and making the beeps of that heart rate monitor pick up a few paces.

'Why would you say that?' his mother asked quietly.

'The whole reason she's gone is because you weren't there. You haven't paid attention to me and Daria for a long time, why would now be any different?'

'That's not fair.'

'No, it's not.'

Daniel's heart continued to beat faster. The beeps of the monitor revealed his anger like a mirror onto his soul.

'I pay attention to you as much as I can,' his mum said, a little tearful now. 'It's not easy being a single mother, Daniel. I have two lives that I need to put together.'

'Except you don't. You're engaged to this other man, and I haven't even met him yet. It seems to me you're not trying to put anything together.'

'I'm not having this conversation again. I listen to you, Daniel. I care. About both of you.'

Daniel shot up in the bed. 'Okay, then let's see. I think The Ogle has Daria.'

There was a pause. A shadow lashed across his mother's face, giving her skin yet another line to add to the others.

'I think The Ogle has Daria,' Daniel repeated. 'I think it took her, and it's hiding her, and it could be that it's killed her, but we don't know. That's why we were there last night. We wanted to find out, and if we could, we wanted to save her. Now we need help.'

Outside the room, Daniel saw the nurse from before approach the glass window and peer through it. He glared at her darkly, hoping that a look alone would stop her from turning the handle. She hesitated for a few moments, then turned back around and decided to give them more time.

'Sometimes I forget how young you are,' said his mum.

Daniel clenched his fists. 'My age has nothing to do with it. I saw The Ogle. I saw it with my own eyes. It took Buster and I think it's taken Daria too.'

'Daniel, you're tired. You're confused. You —'

'I'm not anything. I saw The Ogle's hands in the water, and I know Daria's in there because Terry said —'

'Stop,' his mother said firmly. 'Just stop.'

Daniel reclined on the mattress, shaking his head in disbelief. 'Why won't you listen?'

'Because you're just a kid. You've created a story out of your sister's disappearance, and you think it's going to help you, but it won't. It's just fairy dust.'

'I knew you wouldn't care.'

Out of nowhere, Daniel's mother started towards him, her arms raised. For a moment, it looked like she might hit him, but then she rested both hands on either side of his face, and she stared at Daniel with a fierce, cold intensity.

'I'm your mother, Daniel,' she said plainly. 'Me.'

The door of the hospital room opened, and the nurse stepped back inside. This time, she had a plastic tub in her hand, and she opened it to reveal some swabs and a needle. She put a tourniquet around Daniel's arm and took his blood, and Daniel remained silent.

He and his mother didn't speak about The Ogle after that. They exchanged glances, and that was enough to tell Daniel that any attempt to convince her would be useless. He and Daria had been shrugged off her shoulders years ago, and the only story she believed in now was her own. But there was one person who'd never seen Daniel's stories as fairy dust.

The next time his mum talked to him, it was to say that there was a search for Daria underway in Durwood, and she intended to go to it in just under an hour. She also said that his friends had heard he was awake, and they were on their way to visit, but Daniel didn't intend to stay that long. He had just under an hour to think of a way out.

That way out ended up being pretty simple. Daniel's initial idea involved fashioning a rope out of the leads attached to his chest and shimmying to the car park beneath his window. The second involved him hiding in one of the laundry baskets he'd heard a nurse rolling behind the door. These were fleeting thoughts, however, and he quickly realised the easiest way out would be to get out of bed, put his clothes on (which were waiting for him in a clear plastic bag on a nearby chair), and just walk out of the door. Disappointing. Mundane. But infinitely more practical.

He began phase one of the plan as soon as his mother left the room. Removing the sticky pads from his chest, Daniel leapt out of bed and walked from one end of the room to the other, testing his orientation. It wasn't great, but he wasn't expecting to be completely fighting fit, so he made do with where he was at. After sitting down to put on his clothes, he spent two minutes searching the room for his shoes. They were nowhere to be found, and the more he looked, the dizzier he became, so Daniel passed it off as an insignificant setback and gave up.

He opened the door slightly and peered out, analysing what was waiting for him on the other side. There was a single corridor, with two more doors in front of him and a lift to the right. According to the sign, he was in Ward C of the hospital on the first floor, and he appeared to be the only one, because the corridor was completely deserted. He quickly exited the room and headed straight for the lift, but a doctor turned a corner and spotted him.

'Hey,' he called out, staring over a clipboard. 'Are you supposed to be out of bed?'

Daniel tried to think of something fast. 'Am I supposed to be *in* bed?' he replied.

Clearly that was more confusing than anything the doctor had written on his clipboard. He lowered it and scratched his eyebrows.

'I... are...' he stuttered a little. 'Are you?'

'No,' Daniel said.

He wasn't sure which question he was answering, but he supposed confusion was his best tactic at this point. The doctor frowned. Scratching his eyebrows some more, he turned and walked back the way he came. Perhaps he was going to get someone, or perhaps Daniel had confused him so much, he'd lost his sense of direction. Either way, it gave him another chance to get out, so he walked over to the lift and took it.

Once he was downstairs and in a mass of patients and professionals, it was easy enough to make himself invisible and slip quickly out of the front door. The first thing he saw when he did was the bus stop, which was just outside the first grid of parking spaces. The next bus was only three minutes away, so he waited for six minutes (because of course the bus was late) and then climbed aboard. He told the bus driver he was lost and needed to get to Stone Crest, where his father lived. The driver obliged, no charge applied.

It was midday when the bus arrived at Daniel's stop. In the air, there was still a thick smell of dust and wet grass, but the sun was shining, and any hint of a rain cloud had long since disappeared. He made sure to keep his head down as he got off and started walking.

His dad's house was more of a small, dilapidated bungalow, situated just outside Maker's Mill, where he used to work. It was his fifth place in five years, but because of the low rates he received from his landlord, Mr Barker, who he used to work for, he said he was going to make this one stick. He even said he'd take a summer to fix it up, lest the roof cave in and he was suddenly sifting through rubble to make his tea, but he hadn't done a great job so far.

The stairs to the front door were broken and full of splinters, and the left corner of the building had crumbled so badly, the timber frame was breaking through the brickwork. The windows were dark, almost opaque. The grass below was littered with tiles, some of which had landed in the gutter, causing it to droop about seven inches too low. It was a miserable sight, but Daniel had no choice but to see it. If anyone was going to believe him about The Ogle and Daria, it was his father. He didn't know why (enjoying his ability to tell stories was one thing, actually believing in those stories was another), but Daniel was confident he'd react differently to how his mother did. Perhaps because his mum didn't believe him, and Daniel's dad always jumped at an opportunity to pick his side.

As he climbed the stairs to the door, careful not to let any of the stray splinters pierce his feet, Daniel hoped that today would be no different. He knocked, but silence met him in return, broken only by the craw of a buzzard circling above his head. He knocked again. Then again. But still, there was nothing. Biting his lip, Daniel decided to just try the handle. With his dad owning nothing of any real value, he often left the bungalow unlocked. Sure enough, the door squeaked open as soon as Daniel gave it a push. He poked his head inside and called out,

'Dad?'

The bungalow smelled of old cardboard and burned toast. Immediately to the right, there was the kitchen, where a rusty kettle lay on its side in the sink. A couple of crumb-filled plates were stacked on the drainer. On the table, there was a mug of half-drunk tea and another plate full of baked beans. Next to that, there was an open cabinet, cluttered with nails, bolts, and photographs. His dad's boots and boiler suit were missing, which must have meant he was out, but the television was still on in his bedroom. Daniel could hear it through the walls. Faint, tinny sounds of people talking, accompanied by some music and canned laughter. His dad didn't like to waste electricity, so this alone put Daniel on edge. He walked slowly through the hallway and opened the door.

'Dad?'

The television was in the corner of the room, sitting atop a TV rack, which was also home to a few car magazines and some food wrappers. The bed was in front of it. Grey sheets with a thick, winter duvet, which jerked up and down a bit as Daniel entered.

'Hello?' he said shakily.

And a familiar voice came back. 'Daniel?'

Flinging the duvet onto the floor, Daria spun on the mattress and gave Daniel a great, beaming smile.

'Oh, Daniel! It's *respendent* to see you!'

She jumped off the bed and pulled Daniel into a warm embrace. For a moment, he wondered whether he was dreaming. Like maybe he'd drowned in the fishing hole, and this was just a vision he was having before things went fully black. Except Daria's hug felt real. The touch of her skin, the smell of her hair, the light in her eyes. Everything about her was so real that it simply couldn't be a lie, and yet none of it made any sense. He pushed her off him and grabbed her shoulders.

'Daria! What the hell are you doing here?!'

'You win!' Daria squealed.

'What do you mean, I win?'

'The game! You win the game! Oh, it's been a very long game. Quite tiring.'

The TV in the corner was still yammering away, so Daniel reached over the bed and muted it with the remote.

'Daria, what the hell are you talking about? This isn't a game.'

'Daddy said we were playing a long game of hide and seek. I did think it was a bit *superflewis*.'

'You mean it was Dad who took you?'

'Yes,' said Daria, 'well, he —'

The sound of a door closing made her stop. Daniel swivelled around, his bones stiffening as some heavy footsteps reverberated through the house.

'Oh,' said Daria, 'there he is now. He had to go out to the farm, you see. I wanted to come with him, but he said I might be seen. He's taking this game very seriously. I don't think he likes to lose.'

Daniel listened as the footsteps bounded towards the bedroom. Before he knew it, their dad was standing in the doorway, glaring at the pair of them with his face pale and sweating.

'Dan... Daniel...' he said dazedly. 'What are you doing here?'

'He found me, Daddy!' Daria leapt back onto the bed. 'He won the game because he found me!'

'What's she talking about, Dad?' asked Daniel nervously. 'She said you took her.'

Their father rushed across the room and pulled Daria off the bed. He set her on the carpet before picking up the remote and turning the TV up to max volume.

'Daddy!' Daria covered her ears. 'That's too loud!'

'Go back to watching TV, sweetheart. I'm making it loud so that I'll hear it from the kitchen. Make sure there's no naughty words. Daniel and I are going in there for a quick chat. You just stay right here, you understand me?'

'But the game's over now!' Daria shouted.

'We're going to come up with a new one.' Daniel's dad grabbed his hand, squeezing it so tight, it felt like he'd cut off all the circulation. 'You just stay in here and finish your show.'

Before Daria could argue back, Daniel was yanked out of the room. Rifling in the pocket of his boiler suit, his dad pulled out a key and jammed it into the door lock. He twisted it firmly before hiding it away and racing into the kitchen. Daniel then watched as his dad attempted to make a cup of tea. It was a wild show, soundtracked by the slamming of cupboards and the loud, piercing whistle of the boiling kettle. At one point, he pulled the cutlery drawer so hard it came free of the cabinet, and he cursed as a load of knives, forks, spoons, and cooking utensils were scattered under the table.

'I need you to calm down,' he said skittishly, as if Daniel was the one making tea like a headless chicken. 'I just need you to calm down and take a breath for a moment.'

Daniel backed over to the front door, fully intent on getting out of this house as soon as possible. He'd never seen his dad like this. The man in front of him didn't even seem like his dad at all, rather an imposter wearing the same suit.

Falling to his hands and knees, he picked up the nearest teaspoon, then used it to squeeze a teabag against the side of the mug. His hands were shaking violently.

'I just need you to...' he began speaking again but stopped when he spotted Daniel taking another step backwards. 'Where are you going?'

'I need to tell Mum where Daria is...'

'No, you can't do that.' Daniel's dad flung the teabag into the bin and slammed his mug onto the table. 'You need to wait. You need to... You need to let me explain.'

He pulled out a chair and beckoned Daniel to sit down. Daniel did so hesitantly. For a few seconds, there was nothing to hear except the TV blaring in the other room. Daniel's dad sat down too and dipped his chin towards his lap. The steam from his tea pooled up into his face and broke upon his cheeks.

'I've made a mistake, Daniel. A really terrible mistake.'

Daniel found himself thinking: *Yeah, no shit*. But he didn't vocalise it. He didn't want to vocalise anything, because he had nothing to say. This was all his dad's doing. It was his dad's show, and it called for a monologue, not a conversation. Daniel wanted to know what had happened, why it had happened, and how he had done it. The police had searched this house, after all. They had searched it, and they had questioned him, and his dad, knowing Daria was sitting tight in his own bedroom, had been out on the streets looking for her. He'd fooled everyone, including Daniel. A few minutes ago, he'd been convinced Daria had been taken by The Ogle. He'd risked his life thinking that, and now he felt like the stupidest kid in the world. The Ogle, the blood, the great, nefarious plan to steal his sister and lure him in. It was all just a figment of his imagination. Fairy dust, as his mother so rightly put it. The explanation was far simpler.

And yet it wasn't. There was the surface of things. The shape, the body. Daniel's father had taken Daria. Tick. He got that. But what he didn't get was all the rest of it. The reason and the rationality. The soul and its makeup. That was an answer he couldn't put his finger on, so Daniel sat still and waited for the bones of it.

'It was stupid,' his dad whispered croakily. 'It wasn't me. You know me, Daniel. You've known me all your life. You know something like this isn't me. Except I couldn't help myself. After your mother's engagement, I just felt... Oh, goddamnit, I don't know what I felt.'

He faltered slightly, his head still dipped, and his right hand picking at his left, where there were a speckle of scabs and scars from his work on the farm.

'I know I'm not supposed to say this,' he said after a few seconds. 'I know you're only a kid, but Daniel, I'm in a really fucking bad place.'

Out of nowhere, Daniel watched as his dad crumbled. That was the best way he could describe it. One minute he was looking at his dad. Sad, different, but still together. And the next, it was like Manchester had sent a cricket ball flying into his face. It crumbled in front of him and broke into a thousand tiny pieces. He bent over, sobbing uncontrollably into the tablecloth.

Daniel sat there staring at him, feeling his world go funny for a moment. He'd been aware of everything around him up until now. The plates on the drainer, the cobwebs on the window, his sister in the other room. But as soon as his dad started crying, his vision seemed to narrow. The world around him blurred into obscurity, until there was only one thing left in the centre. His father. He'd never seen him cry before. In a way, he'd thought his father couldn't cry. But he was crying now. Daniel was looking at him and he was crying, and that very fact managed to bend his whole universe.

'It feels like the world is changing.' His dad lifted himself from the table, trying his best to push the words through the weight of his sobs. 'Everything is changing but me. I'm just in the centre of it, being buried in the rising dirt. Normally, that wouldn't bother me. Normally, I wouldn't care, but these last couple of months, something's changed. I feel very far away from myself. Like I'm looking at things from the outside, and I'm seeing my situation, and I'm going... What the hell is going on? What's happening? You realise you're losing everything?'

The tears kept pouring out. They were adamant to come through, to streak down his face and leave their mark on him forever. Scars that could never be unseen.

'You're growing up,' he choked bitterly. 'Your sister is too. Your mother is moving on, and pretty soon, you'll be your own family. That's what I thought I had. That's what I thought I was holding on to. But I realise now, I've just been holding on to broken shards. A window that I helped break. Only now it's being put back together, and I'm gonna be on the other side of it. With nothing. The same old idiot, without the one thing that's made me feel...'

He shook his head, trying to find the words.

'Content. Happy. Accomplished. And what will that do to me? I don't... Well, I know what it will do. It will break me. I've been feeling like this for too long now. Just a shell. Just so empty and scared. Like I can feel it in my chest, this constant anxiety. I'm riddled with it. And it affects everything I do. I can't enjoy things like I used to, I can't do the things I like to do, because it's always there and it's always pulling me. Dragging me down into that dirt and keeping me there. Suffocating me. And I know what will happen when your mother gets married and things completely change. I'll be broken completely, and the anxiety will win because...'

The bubble that had encompassed Daniel rippled slightly. Across the hall, he heard the handle of the bedroom turning and un-turning. The show had finished. The credits were rolling. Daria was calling out for her father, but her father wasn't listening. He was completely inside himself now, yet at the same time, opening himself up, willing to be seen. And Daniel wanted to see him. After a while, the bubble recovered its structure, and the sound of his sister was phased out.

'You remember that day in the goat shed?' his dad asked. 'We spent all that time together. Washing the goats, tending the animals, talking. That was just an ordinary day for you, wasn't it? Nothing really to write home about, right? Except for me...'

He sniffed, shook, then broke down even harder.

'That day on the farm. Those moments. That was the only good thing that happened to me that week.' He held out a finger, his eyes bleary and bloodshot, his chest heaving. 'That was the one ray of light in my life!'

Daniel watched as he slammed his arms down on the table and stuffed himself into them. He didn't know how to react. His world was still a blur, with this weeping mess in the centre. But seeing as this was the only thing he knew, Daniel decided to comfort it. He reached out his hand and placed it delicately upon his father's. It seemed to help. His dad clasped his hand back and looked up. He tried to give him a reassuring smile, but his face was so broken, it came out as more of a grimace.

'Soon, Daniel,' he continued, 'I won't even have that. So I lashed out. I don't even know what I lashed out against. Not your mother. Not anything really. I just went crazy. I took Daria. At first, I thought maybe we'd run away. Like maybe I'd take her to France, and we'd live secretly in the fields somewhere. But then I knew I wouldn't see you again, and it was a completely batshit crazy plan anyway, so that was out the window. So I just took her and hid her here. And I can't even tell you why, because I knew it wouldn't work. I knew she'd be found in a day or two and that would be it, but I still did it.

'Maybe I just wanted to spend time with her, make her know me in the same way you do. Maybe my anxiety has just made me completely irrational and insane, and this is just a cry for help. Maybe everything I've just said to you is just a load of rambled nonsense and you have no idea what I'm saying. I don't know. All I know is that I'm not the person that I was. Your father. Strong and dependable. Ever since things have changed and this anxiety has reared its ugly head, I've been caught in a storm that I can't shelter from. It's crushed me, and I'm sorry for that. I'm sorry.'

Although Daria was still turning on the handle and calling out, the world was silent. Daniel tried to take it all in. He felt at this moment that the monologue should become a conversation. That he should try to offer some words of his own and help his father find himself again. Only nothing was coming. His father hadn't just given him an explanation; he'd completely bled out. Random thoughts, pains and fears soaked the tabletop, and Daniel was entirely without the skills to mop it up. He was just a kid after all. For the first time in his life, he thought to himself: *Perhaps I'll understand when I'm older.*

'I don't know what to say,' he said quietly.

'You don't have to say anything,' his father replied. 'You shouldn't have heard this in the first place. Not this. Not from your dad.'

On that last word, Daniel looked up and realised there was something he wanted to say. It wasn't something he thought he *should* say, because it probably wouldn't help, but it was the truth. And perhaps, in being true, it was a comfort.

'You are my dad,' he said softly. 'You.'

His dad stared at him, and although Daniel couldn't say for sure, he thought he saw something sparkle in his eyes again. At the same moment, he seemed to come in tune with the sound in the hallway. He listened as Daria called out.

'I guess I should let her go, huh? I guess I should let you both go.'

'Won't you get in trouble?' asked Daniel, suddenly afraid of the repercussions of what his dad had done.

'I should think so,' his dad replied. 'But who cares? Maybe some time alone in a cell is what I need. Or what I deserve.'

'But will you get better?'

The question had left Daniel's lips before he could stop it. He scolded himself for being so naive. It was a stupid thing to ask, he knew. It was a kid's question. A kid who could only see in a straight line to the end of things, without any thought or consideration for how hard it was to get there. He knew now more than ever that the way forward was complicated, and most likely, could never be foreseen. So what was the point in asking? It would always be a guess. Something rooted in hope, rather than anything real.

Sure enough, his father chuckled and mumbled tearfully, 'How long is the road to Castletown? The truth is nobody knows. But it's a long road. It's a long road.'

He nodded, agreeing with himself completely about that. Then he stood up and left the room, and when he did so, the bubble was popped. The world around Daniel returned. The chair he was sitting on, the table, the dishes in the drainer, the sun blaring through the window. It all came back.

But different now. All of it different.

THE EVENING, 18 JUNE 2073

The stranger looked emotional. A mesh of sadness and curiosity was etched across his face, which was beginning to go slightly pink in the growing evening light. He'd listened to the story without interrupting once. Not a sound left his lips. He simply absorbed it all, processed it, and Daniel could see the calculation in his eyes.

It was clear that the equation didn't make sense. There was no answer to it, just as Daniel had never found an answer. To be honest, he was a little surprised. He had assumed his equation had been hampered by the fact he was the child, and his father was his father. But it was clear now that even someone on the outside struggled, and perhaps that said something about parenthood as a whole. Daniel didn't believe in God, but parents were close to it. They were the bringers of life, the light in every child's sky, bestowed upon them by stars and nature. And yet, they were fallible. Breakable. Human. As a child, putting a finger on that was almost impossible, and even as a grown up, the hand still had to be forced. All Daniel knew was the same thing he'd told his father all those years ago. He was his dad. *He* was.

'I don't know what to say,' the stranger said eventually.

'It was difficult for me too,' Daniel replied.

He shifted a little in his chair, and Junebug woke up, blinking at her owner with tired affection. She leapt off his lap and walked over to her food bowl, which was covered in shadow now. At this time of the day, when the air was a little cooler and the sun a little less harsh, Daniel would normally sit outside again and listen as the birds went to sleep. But now that he was here in his house, with this stranger, he decided against it. Letting him in once had been hard enough. Letting him in for a second time would be torture.

'So what happened next?' the stranger asked, watching as Junebug lapped up the rest of her salmon pieces.

'If parents are God, then they need their own saviour. Sometimes that can be their children.'

The stranger shook his head. 'I don't understand.'

'I didn't want my dad to go to jail, so I made sure that he didn't. *I* took Daria. I wanted the village to believe in The Ogle. I wanted it to be a story again. A real story.'

The stranger's expression was not too far from what Daniel's father had looked like all those years ago, the first time he'd told him his plan.

'You took the blame?'

Daniel nodded. 'She was in The Ogle House all along. We were looking after her when we weren't on show, joining in with the searches.'

'Your father let you do that?'

'I talked him into it. Us kids can be quite persuasive.'

Daniel hesitated and checked himself. *Us* kids. Daniel hadn't been a kid for a long time now, but somehow the phrase still felt right. There was no doubt that telling this story had placed him into his eleven-year-old shoes, but he hadn't been prepared for how well they would fit. To that extent, telling it was a privilege. One that not many others his age would experience. He looked at the stranger, and for a moment, he felt an odd rush of affection towards him.

'And your friends went along with it?' he asked.

'Of course they did.' Daniel cleared his throat. 'They were my friends.'

The stranger took that in, the equation still going on behind his eyes. 'And that was how it ended? Your father took Daria, and you took the rap. What about what you saw in the fishing hole?'

Daniel couldn't help but chuckle. 'Are you disappointed?'

'I'm not sure.'

'Sometimes the true explanations are the simplest ones. Maybe I blacked out when I hit the water. Maybe that was all just a dream. My vision of The Ogle.'

'Is that what you believed?'

In the corner of the kitchen, Junebug stopped eating and trotted expectantly towards the garden door. While Daniel wasn't willing to go out, it was clear her schedule wasn't going to be tampered with. He stood, let her out, then sat back down.

'Yes,' he said. 'After I found Daria, and what Manchester told us about Terry... that's what I believed. But my summer wasn't over yet.'

He looked at the stranger and prepared to tell the last part of his story. In some ways, it was the hardest part. But Daniel was ready. He had the energy, the willpower, the urge. In other words, he felt young enough.

Chapter Twelve

READ IT AND WEEP

It had been one week since Daria had returned home, and the village of Deanshire looked at Daniel differently now. There were tuts and angry frowns, raised eyebrows and pursed lips. He didn't get sweets for fifty pence less at Bennie's anymore. Everyone in the village, from Mrs Margyle to Champ the Tramp, looked at Daniel like he was a completely different kid. A troublemaker, a liar, a criminal. But that was okay, because he looked at the village differently too.

Ever since that conversation with his dad, Daniel's world had changed. In a way, it had become sharper. Like he saw things more clearly than before. He couldn't quite put his finger on it, but it felt like the village was full of real people with real flaws. He'd always felt a little indifferent towards them, but now he knew his father's plight, and that no one had stepped in to help, it made him angry. It wasn't a kid's job to do that. A kid didn't know how. When they fell down and grazed their knee, they had their parents to kiss it better. But who did their parents have? By all rights, they should have had each other. Their fellow man to lean on and heal their wounds. But clearly not. Daniel's father had told him that taking Daria had been a cry for help, but he shouldn't have had to cry in the first place. A whisper should have done the trick.

Daniel walked through the crowd of village-folk and heard a few whispers coming his own way. Cusses followed him where he went, and while he tried to ignore the perpetrators, they made no such effort. They paid more attention to a kid they wanted to hate than a man — one of *them* — who needed help, and that told Daniel everything he needed to know.

'You'd think there was no punishment.'

Jamie stopped alongside him, and Daniel nodded. He'd been punished, alright. Every Friday for a year, he now had to talk to a community therapist. A withered old crow who scolded him for so much as yawning. As well as that, he had 'community resolution projects' on Saturdays, lasting for four months, and starting with the de-weeding of the church's graveyard. For his parents, they had to be interviewed by social services and had regular meetings with a family support worker, making sure to remind them what a terrible son they had, and how terrible they had been for bringing him up wrong.

Of course, his dad knew the truth, but his mum certainly believed them. She didn't talk to Daniel for four days after he confessed, but on the fifth day, she seemed to think the whole thing was her fault. She hadn't been there enough, and because of this, Daniel's prank had simply been a cry for attention. A last gasp effort to get his mother to look at her family again and realise how much she'd been missing. That was one good thing to come out of all this, Daniel supposed. Ever since Daria had disappeared, his mum had been far more present, and it looked like she intended to be that way from here on out.

'Grubby little liar.'

A low, gurgling voice came from the crowd, but Daniel couldn't tell who said it. They were walking through the high street, approaching the Music on the Meadow fair, which took place on Eastdow Meadow every year on the eighteenth of August. It was approaching six o'clock, so the crowd was getting dense, but this was the only road that was open.

Daniel hadn't really wanted to go this year. If anything, he just wanted to stay in his room and shut the world out with his Walkman, but his friends had forced him to come. No matter what had happened that summer, passing up on candy floss and the chance for some fairground action was apparently impossible.

After two more minutes, Jamie and Daniel squeezed through the crowd and felt grass beneath their feet. The meadow was awash with colourful lights. Children ran from one dodgy-looking ride to the next, coins jangling in their pockets and candy floss beginning to melt onto their fingers. Parents gathered in groups with plastic cups in their hands and expensive-looking sunglasses hooked atop their noses.

A group beneath the ferris wheel was the first to spot Daniel. He couldn't hear what they were saying, but they were pointing and shaking their heads disapprovingly. At the end of the field, there was a large metal stage, with a DJ in the centre fiddling around with knobs, pretending to do something while *Who*

Let The Dogs Out by Baha Men blared out of the speakers. He drowned out most of the barbs, but as Daniel and Jamie made their way further into the centre of the meadow, a few were audible in passing.

'Who let the liar out?'

'Always knew the Ottomans were a bad sort.'

'I hope he goes missing. See who looks for him then.'

They weren't the worst insults in the world. It was still Deanshire, and all the middle-class residents struggled to as much as mutter a swear word, let alone hurl one at a kid. But they still hurt. All Daniel had done was look for his sister, and he looked further and harder than any of these people did. In a way, he wanted to grab them by the collar and spurt out the truth, but any time he thought about doing that, his dad appeared in front of him. Pale, hollow, shaking in that kitchen chair. If putting up with mild animosity meant he could save his dad from jail, then that's what Daniel intended to do. This village had never really liked him in the first place. As far as they were concerned, Daniel and his friends were just a blot on an otherwise unscrupulous portrait. They walked around Deanshire just a little too freely, and the sooner they grew up and realised walls weren't for climbing, the better.

Daniel thought about this as he approached one of those walls in question, using Jamie's shoulder to clamber on top. He pulled Jamie up after him and they took in the scenery. They were sitting on one of the walls of the tennis pavilion, just next to the abandoned courts, where a group of children were playing a game of football. To the left of them, there was a row of food vendors, each tucked inside small, vertical tents, with clouds of steam flowing from their backsides. Hot dogs, burgers, corn on the cob, crepes. Anything that could get your fingers sticky and your belly full, it was all right here on this meadow, and with the number of rides available (right now, Daniel was watching a group of teenagers screaming at the top of the drop tower) it threatened to be here twice.

Daniel soaked in the smells, sights, and sounds, and he tried to force himself to feel less miserable. That became pretty difficult when he spotted Manchester and Curtis. They were walking right in the thick of the crowd, crepes in their hands and a couple of unopened sodas in their pockets.

'Hey, sheep boy,' Manchester shouted over a mouthful of batter and chocolate. 'How does it feel being so close to Baltic Green? Your Ogle senses tingling yet?'

Manchester had been teasing him about The Ogle ever since he'd learned the truth about Daria. Not because he didn't believe in The Ogle (Daniel was pretty sure that he did), but because it apparently proved him right about Terry. Daniel didn't know how that was the case, but he hadn't gone as far as asking him yet. He didn't want to give him the satisfaction.

'Give it a rest, Manchester,' said Jamie as they pulled up beneath their feet.

'Give what a rest?' Manchester spat some toffee chunks onto the wall. 'I saved his life. It's my right to give him a hard time.'

'He's got you there, Daniel,' said Jamie.

'I don't care.' Daniel bent down and tied up a loose shoelace. His eyes were on the carousel now, which was positioned around twenty feet behind the food vendors.

'Oh, cheer up,' said Curtis. 'It was your choice to do this, remember? If it was me, I would have been happy for my dad to be thrown in jail. I probably would've done it myself.'

'The difference is, I actually like my dad.'

'Even after he took your sister and let you take the blame? Sounds like you should hate him.'

'He's going through a hard time,' said Daniel, still staring at the carousel. 'Not thinking straight. I took advantage.'

'And now everyone hates you,' Manchester said happily. 'Job done. Want a bit of my crepe?'

'No, thanks.'

'Has Daria gone along with it?' asked Jamie.

'Sure. She listens to me. To her it's all just a game.'

Jamie laughed. 'She's had an interesting summer. As a matter of fact, we all have.'

As he said this, *Who Let The Dogs Out* started fading away and was replaced with *This Love* by Maroon 5. As if in protest, barks erupted from the tennis courts. Manchester turned, his eyes wide and hopeful, like he expected to see Buster sitting there waiting for him. Instead, what he saw was a black lab, biting and slobbering over the football. The kids kicked him away, and Manchester kicked his attention back to his crepe.

'Still no luck with Buster?' asked Daniel sensitively.

Manchester shook his head. The fishing net had been found washed up on the river bank the morning after Buster was dunked in the water. It was tattered and chewed, like Buster had forced his way out. But there'd been no sign of him yet. The missing posters Manchester and his family had taped up around the village hadn't helped. The only call they'd got turned out to be a sighting of Champ the Tramp, who'd been spotted lying by the bus stop in his fluffy brown blanket.

Daniel hadn't told Manchester about what he'd seen in the fishing hole. After what had happened with his dad, he assumed he'd hallucinated the whole thing. It didn't matter that those hands had looked real — *so real* — if there was a chance it had all happened in his head, he wasn't going to bother Manchester with it. There wasn't a lot he could do with the information anyway.

'He'll show up,' said Curtis, patting Manchester on the shoulder. 'Dogs always like a bit of a run around. He's just getting it out of his system.'

'Getting what out of his system?'

'You know, being free. Having the world at his paws. He'll soon work out Deanshire is a pretty boring place and when he does, he'll come right back home. You just watch.'

'I am watching,' said Manchester.

And Daniel was watching too. But not for Buster. He'd been waiting patiently for a flash of blue hair to emerge from the crowd. And he saw it now. To the right of the carousel. Terry Bantam. Even from this distance, she looked beautiful. Her hair was pulled up into a ponytail, and her shirt was loose and baggy, revealing the tiger tattoo on her collarbone, which sparkled and shone under the fairground lights.

Without saying anything to his friends, Daniel jumped from the wall and rushed towards her. He hadn't been sure if she'd show up. Daniel had visited St Martha's House three times since the incident at the fishing hole, but she hadn't come out of her room once. Part of him wondered whether she was angry at him. Like maybe she blamed Daniel for dragging her into such a dangerous situation, based on nothing but a fanciful story he'd clearly dreamed up. But as Daniel pushed through the crowd and approached her, there was no faking the smile that broke upon her face.

'There he is,' she said cheerfully. 'Thought you might be leading me on again.'

'So you got my note?'

'No, I'm just a psychic — FUCK! SHIT! WANKER!'

Manchester, Curtis, and Jamie skidded to a halt behind Daniel.

'Don't run off like that!' Jamie scolded him breathlessly. 'We thought you might have seen Buster.'

'Look who it is!' Terry beamed at them. 'Nerdy birdy and company.'

'What's she doing here?' asked Manchester, glaring at Terry with that familiar look of spite and loathing.

'I asked her to come,' replied Daniel.

'Why?'

'Don't worry, boogerman. Daniel said you'd need someone to hold your hand on the ghost train. You can't be holding a boy's hand, can you? What would the ghosts think?'

'I'm not going on the ghost train.'

'You don't have to be scared. If any ghosts come near you, I'll just tell them to fuck off. I usually do.'

Manchester tugged Daniel's sleeve. 'Daniel, you don't want her here. She's — OW!' He jumped as Curtis pinched his arm. 'What was that for?!'

'You said you wouldn't tell him,' Curtis hissed.

'Tell me what?' asked Daniel.

But before Manchester could say anything, Terry fell into one of her tics, swearing so loudly that she caught the attention of one of the mums by the carousel. She marched over to them, leaving her little girl stranded on the horse.

'Excuse me! Do you mind not using that language in front of the children?!'

Terry raised a handwritten card that was hanging around her neck.

HEY.
I HAVE TOURETTE SYNDROME.
IF I SWEAR AT YOU, OR SHOVE YOU, OR DO ANYTHING UNUSUAL, THAT'S PROBABLY WHY.
NOT MY FAULT. BLAME MY BRAIN.
PLEASE UNDERSTAND.
CHEERS X

'Read it and weep,' she said once the tics were over.

The mother squinted as she read the note. With an unimpressed huff, she retreated back to the carousel and grabbed the attention of one of the ride attendants.

'Oh, you bitch,' murmured Terry. She turned back to Daniel. 'We should probably move. I don't care about those kiddies learning the F word a few years early, but apparently, I'm the only one. Anyone for dodgems?'

Terry swivelled on her feet and re-entered the crowd. Daniel followed her, then Curtis, then Jamie. Manchester too, only he hung back, his hands in his pockets, and a scowl still plastered across his face.

The next two hours were actually spent having fun. They started in the dodgem rink, where Daniel was able to channel some of his frustrations by crashing into a number of people who'd been looking at him funny. Next, they moved onto the drop tower, where Terry finally felt at home screaming every swear word under the sun along with all the other kids. After that, they bought some sodas from a pop-up stall (only Daniel had to hang back, as they wouldn't serve him), squeezed onto a basket swing, and talked about what ride they should go on next before the fireworks started.

Once they'd made their mind up on the ghost train, they started talking about the fishing hole. But only briefly. On the night of the incident, Terry had run straight to the nearest phone box and called the police, but upon returning to the fishing hole, they'd already been and gone. She'd felt so bad about running away that she'd locked herself in her room and hadn't talked to anyone but her slugs — which, apparently, were all doing well.

Judging by his continuous tutting and subsequent departure to get another crepe, Manchester clearly found this hard to believe. But Daniel didn't care. He was just relieved that Terry didn't think he was stupid. She had every right to pass him off as a foolish kid who had jumped straight to The Ogle conclusion the moment his sister went missing. But not only did she avoid doing that, she seemed to think he was still right about the whole thing.

'So what's our next move with The Ogle?' she said after downing the rest of her Coke.

Daniel almost spat out his. 'How do you mean?'

Over on the stage, the DJ stopped the music and spouted something incoherent into the microphone. Daniel only caught the word, 'fireworks', which he was sure were coming now the sky was growing dark. Terry ignored him completely.

'What, you think just because your dad took Daria, we can just forget about it?'

Jamie scratched the back of his head nervously. 'Uh, yeah, kind of.'

'But we found its home. You were right, nerdy birdy. It's definitely down there.'

Terry pulled herself up on the swing. Her left leg was brushing Daniel's, and despite the fact she'd just thrust the thought of The Ogle back into his head, that was all he could think about.

'Right,' Jamie replied. 'It's just, we don't really need to find it now, do we?'

'What about my parents? I helped you lot when you asked for it. My parents are still gone, but if we find The Ogle, maybe I can find out what happened to them.'

Curtis pulled himself up too and cleared his throat. He was staring at Terry with the same look Manchester had been giving her all evening.

'She's right,' Daniel said, finally getting his attention off the skin contact.

'Daniel,' said Curtis, 'I don't think —'

'I want to go back,' Terry interrupted him. 'I want to try again. We'll just be looking for someone else this time.'

'But how do you suppose we do that?' asked Jamie.

Terry jumped off the swing and twirled back towards them. 'I'm glad you asked, nerdy birdy. Because I have an ace up my sleeve.' She pulled some paper from the waistband of her shorts, flapping it in front of them excitedly. 'I've gotta admit something to you all — Fuck! Wanker! — I didn't come here to go on the rides. I wanted you to see this. A map I found...'

She unfolded the map and lay it down on the grass. From where Daniel was standing, it looked like a load of random lines and wavy, unintelligible text. Only Terry was pointing at it like she'd just found Wally.

'You ever heard that urban legend about the tunnels underneath Deanshire? Apparently, smugglers built them back in the 1700s. A whole underground network that was used to smuggle and hide things like brandy and silk. Lots of people assume it's just a story, but I went to the library and found this. It's a copy of a map drawn up in 1715. According to this, there's supposed to be a tunnel that goes straight under the River Rocker, up near the Cuckoo Line. The same bit we were walking on last week. Come closer, Daniel, look where I'm pointing.'

'I'm not sure that's a good idea,' said Curtis.

But Daniel was already on his feet. 'She's right, though. She helped us when we needed it.'

'Except I don't think she's — Oh boy...'

Curtis stopped as Manchester appeared through the crowd, another crepe in one hand and his fourth Tizer of the evening in the other.

'What's going on?' he asked casually.

'Terry's showing us a map,' Jamie replied. 'She thinks it could lead us to The Ogle.'

Manchester scowled again. 'A map...'

'It's like a piece of paper with squiggly lines,' Terry explained. 'Tells you where things are.'

'I know what a map is.'

'Ah, okay. Well, don't stand too close. I don't want you getting boogers on it.'

Suddenly, Manchester's eyes were locked onto Curtis's, the can of Tizer beginning to dent a little in his grasp.

'Why are you letting this happen?'

'Letting what happen?' asked Daniel.

'You said you wouldn't say anything,' Curtis said again.

But Manchester wasn't listening now. He slammed his crepe down on the swing (splattering Jamie with chocolate, which he gladly mopped up), and turned back to Daniel.

'Screw what I said. Daniel, she's bullshitting you.'

Terry looked up from the map. 'What are you on about, boogerman?'

'I did a bit of research of my own, didn't I? You've only lived here for four years. You were never here as a kid. You never went missing.'

Terry laughed, only it sounded more like she had choked on something sharp and bitter. 'I don't know where you're getting your research from. I — Fuck off! Fuck off! Spoilsport!'

'Spoilsport am I?' Manchester leaned in towards her. 'Why's that then?'

'Fuck off! Fucking little booger-brain with his moppy dog!'

'Correction. *Without* his moppy dog. Buster is gone because of you.'

Daniel shook his head, confused. 'I don't understand.'

'She lied to you, Daniel. I don't know why. Maybe she wanted friends, or maybe she's sick in the head. But she lied. The fishing hole. The Ogle. All of it.'

Terry leapt onto her feet. 'FUCKING LIAR! THAT'S WHAT I AM! FIND THE OGLE! FIND DARIA! NO GOOD, ROTTEN LIAR!'

'For once,' said Manchester, 'her Tourette's is telling it exactly like it is. She played a game with us, Daniel. She didn't go missing. She didn't lose her parents.'

'PROVE IT, BOOGERMAN!'

'With pleasure.'

Manchester reached into his back pocket and pulled out a folded piece of paper of his own. As he unfurled it, Daniel could see photographs with text underneath. Manchester held it out and pointed to the one in the middle. Terry Bantam, a little younger, perhaps eleven or twelve, with two people standing either side of her. A middle-aged man with a moustache and thinning hair, and a woman, just a few inches taller than her, wearing a pinstripe suit and smiling. In Terry's hands was a painting of what looked like the Deanshire high street. Daniel read the caption.

ESTHER NICHOLS BANTAM (13) WINS SECOND PLACE IN DEANSHIRE'S ART EXHIBITION.

Esther Bantam, having only just moved to Deanshire this year, delighted judges with her stunning depiction of the village's high street. In the words of head judge, Gloria Ankleman, "Esther has communicated an immediate connection with our little village, portrayed so effectively with bold, blustering brushstrokes and an outstanding use of colour." She was joined by her mother and father, Argus and Julia Bantam, and accepted the award as runner-up to Arthur Hickman ("Water Light in the Morning", see pg.3)

'Read it and weep,' said Manchester.

And sure enough, Terry Bantam began to weep. Tears streamed down her cheeks and her muscles twitched and jolted, like she was being repetitively zapped by sharp electric shocks. She looked at Daniel pleadingly, but Daniel was still staring at the picture.

'Is it true, Terry?'

'I don't...' Terry began, but then she lurched again. 'Fuck off! Fuck off! — I didn't mean to — Shit!'

Daniel shook his head. 'Everything you said about The Ogle. About my sister. Why the hell —'

'Because she's a psycho,' Manchester answered for him. 'Just another psycho from St Martha's House, coming up with a story and playing it out for her own amusement.' He refolded the magazine snippet and put a hand on Daniel's shoulder. 'Except she used your story. Your pain.'

'I didn't use him.' Terry fought back. 'It wasn't a game — Fuck off! Ooh, strawberries! Yum, yum!' She whistled beautifully, and the tears fell onto her lips, making them shine like she was wearing gloss.

'Did you go missing?' Daniel glared at her. 'Were you telling the truth about The Ogle?'

There was a beat. Terry shivered and spasmed again.

'No,' she said. 'It wasn't the truth. I'm sorry.'

Behind her, the world lit up in a blaze of colour. Red, purple, green, and blue. Splashes of light erupted onto the canvas of the sky, making it sizzle, and shine, and pop. Yet none of them were watching. They were all staring at Terry. Her pale face, her dark eyes, her hair, which now looked far less blue under the glow of the fireworks. They stood there quietly, waiting for her to say something. Only nothing else came. Terry simply wept and shook, then reached out to Daniel.

'I didn't...' She wiped her eyes. 'It wasn't a game. I just didn't want you to... I just thought...'

Daniel stepped away before she could touch him. He looked down at the map again. 'What's this then? Isn't this map another game?' He grabbed the snippet from Manchester's hands. 'What's this?'

'I didn't — Fuck off! Fuck off, fuck off!'

'Your parents aren't missing. They're right here.'

'They probably carted her off to the loony bin themselves,' said Manchester. 'I don't blame them.'

'I'm sorry I lied,' said Terry. 'I... I...' She was trying to control herself, but the tics were still coming. 'I'm sorry but — Strawberries! — I still want to be your friend — Strawberries in a hat, gonna fucking mash 'em! — Please don't leave me.'

'If you want to be our friend,' said Daniel, 'why would you do this?'

'Fucking fun, wasn't it? Stupid little kids! Fucking hilarious! Strawberries! Woohoo! Fuck off!'

Terry clapped a hand over her mouth. With the other, she grabbed her card. Daniel's gaze flickered down to it. Her fingers covered everything but one line. *Please Understand*. And Daniel, indeed, understood. He knew what she was now. Manchester had been right all along. In front of him, Terry's hand lowered as she continued swearing, calling them as many names as she could before rounding it all off with a loud, tortured,

'FUCK OFF!'

And Daniel looked at her sadly. 'Gladly,' he said.

Then he turned away and his friends turned with him. They walked out of the park, leaving Terry alone and crying under the dark, fading colours of the summer sky.

A horrible, deathly silence followed them on their way home. The time was eight-thirty, and the streets of Deanshire were still bustling, so the boys decided on a different, quieter route. Through Wealding Woods, which would take them onto Baltic Green, a spot that had become far less terrifying now that summer was ending.

Daniel spent most of the journey staring down at his feet, riling against a hard, heavy stone which was pressing onto the floor of his stomach. He'd known Terry for just over a week, but even so, he felt like he'd lost someone dear to him. Daniel had never really fancied a girl before. As a matter of fact, he wasn't sure why anyone *would* fancy a girl. But the butterflies he got when he'd been around her had changed all of that. He had fancied her. He'd adored her. But adoring Terry was like adoring the moon in the darkness of childhood. Every kid was scared of the dark. That's why they kept the light on when they went to bed. But the darkness outside was different to the darkness inside. The moon was bright and claimed to be a protector, but really, there was no light. When you got lost in the night, the moon turned out to be just a flat, faraway bulb that you couldn't even poke. It was untouchable. It was meaningless. It was a lie. And that's what Terry had been. She had shone, she had sparkled, but she had lied. And Daniel, who was now so used to seeing past the surface of things, couldn't see her any other way.

He didn't know why. He didn't want to know why. All he wanted to do was get home and put it all behind him. Start again, in effect, and forget this summer had ever happened. But as the four boys converged onto Baltic Green, he quickly realised that wasn't going to happen.

'You know,' said Manchester, breaking the silence. 'I'm starting to think the whole Ogle thing is just a sham. Something to keep us kids in check.'

He didn't say anything else. Perhaps he didn't need to, because all of them were beginning to think the same thing. Daniel knew they'd taken it too far. They'd believed in a way they should never have believed, and liars like Terry had egged them on. Had some fun. Mocked and played with them. Even the blood theory was crazy now that he considered it. Daniel had left his blood at the house, yes. But Buster had been cut on his paw, and he'd left far more blood than Daniel had. If Daniel had been identified and targeted because of his blood, why wasn't Buster?

He was just thinking this as they passed The Ogle House. All four of them glanced towards the entrance — in a way, because they wanted to put it to rest. They wanted to see the house, and the walls, and the door, and the windows, and they wanted to see it as ordinary. Mundane.

If they were going to turn over the page and start again, then this would be their full stop. But instead of seeing nothing, they saw something. A large, black mass, shining in the dying sun and dangling from the pergola. Buster the dog. Hanging on a rope by the neck, just the way Daria's teddy had hanged from the fishing line. Dead and dripping. With a warning painted in red above him, like the epitaph of a tombstone.

VISIT ME AGAIN.
I DARE YOU.

And it became clear to Daniel then that his summer would never be forgotten. Not one breath. Because it remembered. This summer and the things in it. Everything remembered. So he would remember too.

THE EVENING, 18 JUNE 2073

Daniel watched as the sun dissolved into a new colour. It hanged in the sky like a slow firework, turning from yellow to orange, until it fell towards the horizon and shattered through the gaps in the trees. This was the same dance it did every evening. The same display. Only now it felt different. In a way, it felt like the last firework from that night, sixty-nine years ago. A firework that had danced and dived a thousand times, yet was nearing its finale, finally, now the story had been told, falling into tiny particles and breaking into the night.

This evening was over, and that evening was too. Because Daniel wouldn't think on it anymore. The memory was done and dusted, folded away and put neatly in a drawer, where it would remain in the dark forever, never to be read again. He'd been able to blow the dust off, and he was happy about that. But he knew the next layer of dust would build until the ink grew faint, and the paper crumbled, and the memory was nothing more than dust itself, to be blown into the wind like ashes from an urn. And that was sad. He'd never really known that day was still with him. That night. That whole summer. The pages had been there in the back of his mind, and he thought, now that he knew better, he should have read them more. But when all was said and done,

'That was how it ended.'

And he knew, really, that the end in question couldn't be more complete.

'I'm so sorry that happened,' the stranger said sombrely. He was sitting in the chair opposite Daniel, slouched all the way back as if the tale had just given him a straight-right.

'We got through it,' Daniel replied.

'I don't know how.'

'No. It was a terrible thing to see. But I saw it with my friends by my side. My best friends. That made all the difference.'

'What about Terry?'

'What we saw didn't vindicate her. Not to Manchester. Not to any of us.'

'You didn't talk to her?'

'No. She still lied. She still did that.'

The stranger wiped his mouth, still in shock. Underneath the table, Daniel could see his leg jerking up and down. Junebug, who had just returned from her outdoor wandering, was staring at it. She had the same look in her eye that she wore before attacking her scratching post, and for a moment, Daniel considered whether he should tell him. But he decided to let things play out. The stranger had already received too much affection from his cat. Perhaps a little aggression would provide a neat balance.

'But it couldn't have ended there,' said the stranger adamantly. 'There are too many questions.'

Daniel rubbed his hands and contemplated. 'We were kids,' he said. 'And we had childhoods to live. We went back to school. We did our exams. We learned to put it behind us. Not forget. We could never do that. But if that was our warning shot, we didn't want to know what the shot itself would feel like.'

The stranger stopped shaking his leg. Junebug plodded away disinterestedly, and despite himself, Daniel felt a tinge of disappointment.

'But I know this is just the beginning of the story. There's more. The summer of 2005. I want to know what happens next.'

'This *is* the end,' said Daniel firmly. 'The summer of 2005... Well, that's a whole other story.'

A moment passed. Then a flicker of a smile flashed across the stranger's face.

'One that you're going to tell.'

'Is that an order?'

'Yes. With a please on top.'

'So polite.'

Junebug slipped through the gap in the door and disappeared into the hallway. Daniel stood. He stretched his back and heard a click. He wiped his eyes and felt some of the dust still there from the morning. His head felt heavy. He dragged himself over to the kitchen counter, where he began making his traditional cup of hot cocoa, which he always made before bed.

'You don't have to be, you know,' he said with his back turned. 'I know what you're doing here. I know why I have to tell you all this. My story. My summers. The consequences of what happened. I remember.'

The stranger remained silent, so Daniel turned to him.

'The O' So Polite Stranger. Tell me, is it an act?'

'Are you asking the questions now?'

'Like I said, I don't have to. When we get to the last page, I know what's coming. I know you're here to kill me.'

The stranger stared at him, his pale, green eyes dancing in the soft light. 'Yes,' he said politely. 'Yes, I am.'

Daniel nodded. He'd known this was the case from the moment the stranger's car had pulled up on his driveway, but it was still jarring to hear it confirmed. In a weird way, it was almost a relief. Like things were out in the open now. Every secret was being told. He turned back to the counter and poured his cocoa into a new mug.

'But if you don't mind, my death can wait. My story too. Until the morning.'

The stranger stood and wrapped his fingers around the neck of the chair. 'I'll stay the night,' he said conclusively.

'You're welcome to.'

Daniel picked up his mug and shifted towards the doorway. He supposed he was being rude, not offering the stranger a bed or a night-time drink of his own. But he rather thought he didn't need to. All the invitations had been made and had rested, right here in this house, and by this point, it belonged to the stranger just as much as him. Still, he wondered if an explanation was in order.

'It's just,' he said, turning, 'it takes it out of you. Talking all day. Reminiscing. It's exhausting. But it's exhilarating too. Bad things happened back then, it's true. In some ways, it was the worst of times. But in other ways, it was the best. And I can't quite work out why. Perhaps it's this distance. Or perhaps it's just who I was. Who I was with. There was happiness there, now that I look back. If you can't see it yet, you will. And I can feel it now, just by saying it out loud. That vitality. That beating heart. I haven't felt this young since...'

'Since...?'

Daniel thought about it, trying to find the words. 'Since I was young,' he said after a few seconds. Then, with a slight nod of the head, he turned and opened the door.

'Goodnight, Daniel,' the stranger said behind him.

But Daniel didn't say it back. He was done talking. With old legs, he hobbled up the stairs, taking them one at a time. He brushed his teeth and washed his face, as he usually did. He topped up his pills and looked in the mirror. He blinked and breathed. He examined and thought. Then he tucked himself into bed, the mug of hot cocoa resting on his lap. He looked out of the window at the setting sun.

He only drank half of his cocoa before placing it on the bedside table and closing his eyes, and to his surprise, sleep took him quickly.

He didn't dream about the summer of 2004. As he'd said to the stranger, that story was over now. He dreamt about the next season. The next summer. Everything that was still to be told, and the memories that were yet to be relived. He would have called it a nightmare, but it wasn't that, because he saw his friends again. He felt the heat of the sun, the kiss of the wind, the touch of dried grass.

He was lying in bed, but he was dozens of years away. A bundle of youth. A jewel in summer. And he shone.

***The Book Of The Summer* continues...**

MORE FROM EDGAR D JACKSON

Seeing Dead **(2024)**

The Secret Cuckoo Cabaret Club **(2025)**

For a sneak preview of The Book Of The Summer: Season Two, visit the IolandaPress website and sign up to the IolandaPress newsletter.

www.iolandapress.com